What the
Gho

"I love this book! Kids will strongly relate to, and absolutely love, the cast of characters in this exciting mystery. It makes scientific concepts exciting and the scientific method relevant. Like the characters in the book, readers will be encouraged to follow their curiosity, complete tasks and reach goals. The book will certainly pique young readers' interest in emerging scientific fields."
—Renee Anderson, Curriculum and Professional Development Specialist, Illinois Mathematics and Science Academy

"An easy read with a powerful message. This book creatively blends humor and gripping suspense with chemistry, physics, robotics, biology, mathematics and technology. The kids exhibit fear, anxiety, cooperation, communication and compassion—all while utilizing the scientific method. This book should be required reading for all our students and faculty. Science saves the day in this exemplary book!"
—Kamaal Khazen, Dean of Applied Sciences, De La Salle Institute, Chicago, IL

"I loved this novel and believe most readers of any age will, too. It's a great adventure with an educational theme!"
—Piers Anthony, science fiction and fantasy author

"I heartily recommend this adventure in scientific thinking!"
—Ann Druyan, co-writer of the *Cosmos* TV series and wife of the late Carl Sagan

"I especially love that girls are key members of the League. They will inspire and spark interest in girls to explore STEM careers."
—Naiyma Houston, Founder and Director, Upper Hand to College, Ventura, CA

"A great book for mystery enthusiasts and science geeks of all ages, but especially middle grades. The characters are diverse and include smart girls (and boys) who understand the power of inquiry. Readers will be captivated by the entertaining story—and, all the while, they'll be learning how useful science and math can be... even for kids!"
—Diane Dexter, Central Library Services, Manhattan-Ogden School District, Manhattan, KS

The League of Scientists

Ghost in the Water

Science, Naturally®
Washington, DC

First print edition • November 2014
E-book edition • November 2014

Paperback ISBN 13: 978-0-9700106-2-9 • ISBN 10: 0-9700106-2-1
E-book ISBN 13: 978-0-9700106-1-2 • ISBN 10: 0-9700106-1-3

Published in the United States by:
Science, Naturally! LLC
725 8th Street, SE
Washington, DC 20003
202-465-4798 / Toll-free: 1-866-SCI-9876 (1-866-724-9876)
Fax: 202-558-2132
Info@ScienceNaturally.com
www.ScienceNaturally.com

Distributed to the book trade by:
National Book Network
Toll-free: 800-462-6420 • Fax: 800-338-4550
CustomerCare@nbnbooks.com • www.nbnbooks.com

Teacher's Guide available at www.ScienceNaturally.com

Library of Congress Cataloging-in-Publication

Ghost in the water. -- First print edition.
pages cm. -- (The league of scientists ; 1)
Summary: "John Hawkins is in yet another new school as he begins the 7th grade. His life would be just fine except for the fact that Dowser, the school bully, has it out for him. Things change when his passion for robotics lands him an invitation to be a part of a secret club. John joins Malena, Hector, Natsumi, and Kimmey as the newest member of the League of Scientists. Together, these friends pool their knowledge of biology, technology, logic, and chemistry to unravel the mysteries that haunt their quiet town of East Rapids. The League is in a race against time to solve the secret of the ghost who is terrorizing the middle school pool right before the swim meet against East Rapids' biggest rival."-- Provided by publisher.
Audience: Ages 10-14.
Audience: Grades 7 to 8.
ISBN 978-0-9700106-2-9 (pbk.) -- ISBN 978-0-9700106-1-2 (ebook)
1. Science--Juvenile literature. 2. Science--Methodology--Juvenile literature. 3. Scientists--Juvenile literature.
Q163.G59 2014
500--dc23

10 9 8 7 6 5 4 3 2 1

Schools, libraries, government and non-profit organizations can receive a bulk discount for quantity orders. Please contact us at the address above or email us at Info@ScienceNaturally.com.

Printed in the United States of America.

Supporting and Articulating Curriculum Standards

Science, Naturally books
address two dimensions of the
Next Generation Science Standards:
Disciplinary Core Ideas and
Cross-Cutting Concepts.

All Science, Naturally books align with
the Common Core State Standards.

The content also aligns with
the math and science
standards laid out by the
Center for Education at the National Academies

Articulations to these, and other standards,
are available at
www.ScienceNaturally.com.

Teacher's Guide Available!

Expand and extend the learning experience
with our teacher-written study guide.
Download at www.ScienceNaturally.com

Don't Try This at Home!

Although most of the science in this book is accurate, the author has taken some liberties with the facts in order to make the story more exciting.

Dry ice can be dangerous if stored or used improperly. It kills cells if it comes into contact with skin. Handling it improperly or swallowing it is dangerous. It sublimates into carbon dioxide gas and lowers the percentage of oxygen in a room—this can cause problems if a room is not properly ventilated. It is not flammable, but, when stored in a sealed container, poses an explosion hazard.

Fluorescein, whether used topically, orally and/or intravenously, can cause adverse reactions, both mild and serious. Adverse reactions include nausea and hives, but acute hypotension, anaphylaxis, and anaphylactic shock, causing cardiac arrest and sudden death have been seen.

We strongly recommend that you do not duplicate any of the experiments in this book. Any experimentation is done at your own risk. The publisher and authors are not responsible, and expressly disclaim all liability, for any events that occur as a result of trying to duplicate experiments described in the book.

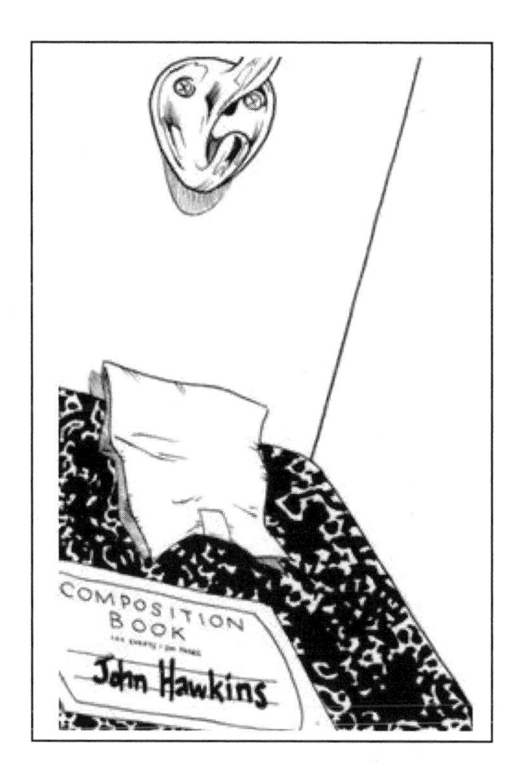

CHAPTER 1

As the bell rang, signaling the end of the school day, John headed down the hall and put his books in his locker. Unlike the other students, he was in no rush. Malena had called a League meeting for this afternoon. But instead of meeting at the Lab like they usually did, she was having everyone meet on the fourth floor of the school, in room 14.

The room was dark and empty when John walked in. *Strange,* he thought, *normally, there's a teacher still in here from last period*. He didn't have much time to figure it out because suddenly the lights flickered on. Malena Curtina stood behind him in the doorway, backpack in hand.

"Are you ready to go?" she asked him.

"Go? Go where?"

"Why, to the secret location, of course! Did you really think we would meet in the school? Anyone could be watching," she said in the most serious tone she could muster. John, however, could see a small smile tugging at her lips and knew that she was trying to scare him.

Walking past Malena and out the door, he asked, "Where are we going?"

"If I told you, then it wouldn't be a secret, now would it? she responded, as she dashed past him. "Race you down the stairs!"

John sprinted to catch up, pushing himself to make it to the front entrance before her.

"And the winner is … JOHN! The crowd is going wild," John yelled as soon as he made it to the sidewalk. He collapsed on the grass to catch his breath while Malena walked over to him.

"Well it wouldn't be nice of me to beat you on such a special day," she huffed.

"Special day?" John asked, confused. "What's so special about today?"

"You'll see," Malena called. "Come on, we don't want to be late."

Malena held out her hand. John took it, and she hoisted him to his feet. They walked quietly for a few minutes until John broke the silence. "Is it usually this slow in the case department for the League?" John asked.

"No," Malena replied, "it's really strange. It's almost like someone's making sure there aren't any mysteries."

***

In a dark room on the fourth floor of East Rapids Middle School, a shadow stood in front of a window. It moved away. It had seen enough. It had heard enough. It had watched enough.

***

"Surprise!" everyone yelled as John walked into Ruby's Supreme Frozen Delights with Malena.

Too shocked for words, John just looked around the room at all his friends.

"Welcome, *tomodachi*, to your surprise party!" Natsumi announced, gesturing to the room around her.

"Surprise party? Surprise for what? My birthday's still six months away."

"The party's to mark when you joined the League. It's your anniversary. It's been two months," Kimmey stated proudly.

"Wow, thanks guys!" John said, a grin spreading across his face. "Natsumi, what does *tomodachi* mean?"

"*Tomodachi* means "friend" in Japanese," Natsumi replied as she got up to get some green tea ice cream. She topped it off with gummy bears and peanut butter pieces, creating her own special *dezaato*.

"Well, you may be a *tomodachi* to her, but you are an *amigo* to me," Hector laughed, clapping John on the shoulder.

"Are you guys going to eat that ice cream or sit there chatting all day?" Malena teased as she scooped a spoonful of *soursop* sherbet, her favorite flavor, into her mouth.

"If you put it that way, I guess I'll eat my ice cream—just as soon as I concoct the perfect combination of toppings," Hector answered as he poured banana chips, chocolate brownies and macadamia nuts into his bowl of *lúcuma* sorbet, a fruity treat that always made him happy.

"Hey, leave some sprinkles for the rest of us," Kimmey joked, pushing him out of the way so she could reach the toppings for her ice cream.

"You're one to talk. Do you really need to add brownies to your Double Chocolate Chip Cookie Dough?" Hector replied, while watching John fill his cup. "John, *mi amigo*, you have awesome taste in friends, but when it comes to ice cream, you are so boring."

"You just don't appreciate the delicious simplicity of Vanilla," John shot back, "Rich. Creamy. Perfect."

Everyone gathered around, enjoying their ice cream. Soon, each of their faces had splotches of fudge and sprinkles, but none of them cared. As they were finishing up their sundaes, Kimmey's father arrived and took a picture of them together. It was to replace the old photo back at the Lab.

***

The next day at school, John was sitting in Mr. Elinger's Algebra class when, from the corner of his eye, he saw something small and round flying toward his face. In that split-second, John knew both what it was and who it came from. Unfortunately, this knowledge did not prevent the spit wad from slamming into his cheek. Wet and slimy, it slid down John's face and onto the floor.

John looked down at the disgusting blob and nudged it with his shoe. There was more saliva this time. He looked around the classroom and caught Dowser smiling maliciously from three rows away. John turned back toward the front of the room with a quiet sigh. He wasn't angry or even upset. He was just tired. Whenever these things happened at his old school, John's mother would tell him to ignore the bully. "A bully needs a reaction. If you ignore him, he'll leave you alone." It was good advice, John had to admit, but not for someone like Dowser.

Dowser was almost double the size of John, and his hands were as big as John's head. He didn't seem very smart, but that may have been because he never paid very much attention in class. On homework assignments and tests, it was more common for Dowser to use his intimidating size to cheat rather than create anything of his own.

The only class Dowser ever paid attention in was the HTML class he had with John during fifth period. Only a couple of weeks after John moved to this new school, his HTML teacher held a competition for the best website. Dowser's was pretty good—in fact, so good the whole class had been speechless. No one knew Dowser had it in him, or that there was something he felt strongly enough about to apply himself.

However, much to his surprise, Dowser didn't win the competition. John did. Ever since, Dowser held a grudge against him. Dowser didn't pay attention in that class anymore. He also took all his hurt and insecurities out on John every chance he got.

When Dowser first started tripping John in the hallways and firing spitballs at him in class, John tried to ignore it. After all, bullies were nothing new to him. Usually, they stopped after awhile or just fired insults whenever they were around their friends. John could handle that. What he couldn't handle, what he couldn't understand, was Dowser's persistence. Sometimes, Dowser even chased John home from school for no other reason than because he could.

John had tried talking to him, but Dowser just snickered. Sometimes, when Dowser was chasing him, John thought about turning around quickly and giving him a big shove. But of course, that would never happen. Dowser was big and athletic, a powerful forward on the East Rapids Middle School basketball team. His spiky blond hair and ropy neck made him even scarier to look at. John, on the other hand, was small and skinny, his bones and joints jutting out from his body at weird angles.

John knew that someday Dowser's spit wads, shoving, and chasing would come to an end. The question was *how* to make that happen. Dowser was like a simple robot programmed with only one command: *Get John Hawkins.*

"John, are you paying attention?"

John flicked his eyes away from Dowser. Mr. Elinger stood in front of the class, one hand on his hip. His eyes were big and his cheeks were pink. He got that way maybe once a week and today it was John's turn to feel the wrath.

"Yes," John said automatically, his face flushing a deep red.

"Then you can tell me what I just said, right?"

John turned his eyes toward the desk, and began tapping his left leg nervously.

"Um ... You were asking what the first step is to solve the equation 6x + 7y = -9."

"So what's the answer?"

"Uh ..."

Mr. Elinger breathed out loudly through his nose and sighed, "That's what I thought. See me after class."

John had known the answer, but was too humiliated to say anything. As Mr. Elinger turned back to the board, John heard a snort of laughter. Face burning, he didn't lift his head. It wasn't hard to guess who had laughed.

***

John stayed after class. Mr. Elinger assigned him extra work and gave him a lecture on paying attention, though John's mind started to wander during the scolding itself. He wasn't trying to be rude—it was just the only way he could cope. As he walked out of Mr. Elinger's class, Hector caught up with him.

"*¿Que pasa?* I see Dowser's up to his usual stunts."

"I'm fine," John muttered. "Sad as it is to say, I'm used to this."

"You shouldn't put up with being bullied. Middle school is hard enough as it is," Hector said as he walked toward his class. "Anyway, I gotta run. *¡Hasta luego!*"

John had to agree. Being bullied was not something he wanted in his day-to-day life. He wouldn't complain though; because while being at East Rapids meant dealing with Dowser, it also meant that he had actual friends for the first time in years. In the past, John had been a loner. He didn't have any brothers or sisters and his mom's shift often didn't end until just before he went to bed. His dad wasn't in the picture; he had left when John was still a baby. As a result, John had a hard time getting close to people. He was always afraid of getting left behind. Plus, every time his mother broke up with another boyfriend, she and John would pack up their things and move to a new town. The longest John had ever stayed in one school was three years. After the first couple moves, John gave up trying to make friends. It took a lot of energy and he was tired of saying goodbye. Instead, he spent his free time hidden away in his room tinkering with technology.

There was something nice about his robot kits and electronic gadgets. They only did what they were told, and there was no way for them to leave him behind. Before, he spent most of his time building and tweaking. Now that he had real friends, he still built things, but usually they were for cases the League was working on. Being recruited for the League was one of the best things that ever happened to him. He finally felt like he belonged.

As John rushed to get to Ms. Heida's class before the bell, he thought back on the day that he met his friends in the League of Scientists and the first case he helped them solve.

***

It had been a day worse than most. Dowser was being particularly vicious in his attacks, and John was beyond tired of it all. He had to stay behind in Mr. Elinger's class to turn in corrections on an assignment, and it meant that he had to dash to history. John hurried to his locker, bumping against streams of students hurrying to get to class. He didn't want to be late and he still had to get upstairs.

He yanked open his locker, his hands still shaking from the scolding that Mr. Elinger had given him. When he looked at his bookshelf, the shaking stopped.

A folded piece of red paper sat on top of his book pile. From the crumpled edges, it looked like someone had shoved it through his locker's ventilation grille.

John stared at it a moment before looking up and down the hall. In the mass of students, no one was paying attention to him. He grabbed the paper and shoved it inside his backpack. Checking to make sure he had his history book, he ran for the stairs.

Nearly out of breath, he made it to his class just before the bell. He sat in the last row to avoid attention and pulled out his textbook. He left it closed on his table and slid the bright red paper underneath. He wanted more cover before he opened the message.

"Sit down, everyone," called an authoritative voice from the back of the room. John jerked his head up just as Ms. Heida skirted past his desk. She stopped at the projector in front of the chalkboard and turned back around to stare at her students. "Kimmey, will you hit the lights?"

John watched a pretty blonde girl rise from her desk. He noticed that she looked older than a typical seventh grader as she moved towards the light switch. Once the lights were turned off, John's attention was drawn to the glowing projection.

"Today, we'll be talking about the Egyptian pharaoh Khufu," Ms. Heida said. "Khufu built the Great Pyramid. You've probably seen photographs of it. It's the largest one in the world." She clicked her remote and the image of a pyramid dissolved to show its interior. An intricate drawing showing many rooms and passages appeared on the screen.

"Even today, experts don't know exactly what all the rooms and passages were for. Some held treasure and, yes, maybe a mummy or two. Some might have been passageways allowing the pharaoh's *Ka,* or spirit, to escape the pyramid after burial."

John normally loved this stuff, but today he was too busy thinking about the red piece of paper to pay attention. He opened his textbook slowly. Then, holding his breath, he slid the mysterious note out from beneath his textbook, placed it on top of the open book, and began to read:

<u>We need to talk</u>

001	0001
010	1111
011	0110
100	1010

This was a puzzle—a secret message. Who gave it to him, and why?

"We need to talk," John read quietly and felt a thrill. He looked again at the numbers. Were the numbers themselves a message? The zeros and ones didn't appear to represent letters.

A substitution cipher? A Caesar cipher? Binary?

Binary.

John loved electronics and building robots. The process was more than just "Bolt wheel A to axle B," he still had to tell the robot what to do. He'd first begun programming robots with beginner kits. They were easy to figure out—the robots were programmed with a series of pictures. For example, a big green arrow meant "drive forward" and a red "X" meant "stop."

The first language of all robots and computers was binary. All electronic brains knew binary; for that reason, he'd been working very hard to learn binary.

He squinted at the numbers and bit his pen. Quietly, he slid a notepad from his backpack, glancing up to make sure Ms. Heida hadn't noticed. She was tracing the path of a pyramid tunnel on the projector, talking about airflow… or something.

"One, two, four, eight, sixteen, thirty-two, sixty-four, one hundred twenty-eight..." John muttered the sequence to himself. Starting from the right side of each group, John assigned each digit a number from that sequence. Then he multiplied each digit by the assigned number and added everything together.

The first group of three numbers, "001," was easy:
(4 x 0) + (2 x 0) + (1 x 1) = 1

The second group of three, "010," was similar:
(4 x 0) + (2 x 1) + (1 x 0) = 2

Binary has been tricky at first, but it got simpler once you knew the formula and had time to practice it. John did so frequently.

Head down, he furiously scrawled calculations, glancing up occasionally to make sure Ms. Heida wasn't watching. When he finished, he read the results:

1	1
2	15
3	6
4	10

John stared at the numbers. They still didn't make any sense to him, but something about them seemed familiar.

He began to scribble notes on another piece of paper. After a moment, he looked from his notes to the message and made the connection. He straightened up with a jolt.

The message was his afternoon class schedule. The algebra class he'd come from, where he had been spitball'ed by Dowser, was on the first floor, in Room 1. Ms. Heida's history class was on the second floor, in Room 15. His last class of the day was science on the third floor, in Room 6.

Floor 1, Room 1
Floor 2, Room 15
Floor 3, Room 6
Floor 4, Room 10

Someone knew where he was. Someone was watching him.

Since John had no reason to be on the fourth floor after his last class on the third floor, he knew that had to be where he was supposed to meet the note's author.

John had no idea who might want to talk to him or why. He'd only been at East Rapids Middle School for a couple of months and he hadn't made any friends. It always struck him as ironic that it was so much easier to make enemies. Making friends was a complicated process; it was hard and it was emotionally risky. Rather than make himself vulnerable, John kept his head down, did his schoolwork, and had fun at home with electronics and robot designs. The fact that someone wanted to talk to him came as a complete surprise.

Is it a prank? Somebody playing a joke? Maybe Dowser?

He didn't think so. It didn't feel like a prank, and Dowser's methods were anything but subtle. At any rate, this was a mystery he really wanted to solve. After his final class ended, he'd sprint up to the fourth floor and see who, or what, was waiting for him in Room 10.

***

Getting through science class was agony. The subject never interested him very much even though Mr. Steinhacker had sat him down earlier in the semester and explained how living things have a lot in common with robots. Human cells, for example, have their own power supply (the mitochondria) and a control unit (the nucleus); they move around (with flagellum); and like a robot's body, the cell's cytoskeleton and membrane holds everything together.

But John didn't care, especially not right now. He couldn't think about anything except the note. He looked up to make sure no one was watching. As usual, Malena Curtina dominated the questions and answers. She sat in the front row and usually John couldn't see much of her except for her braided black hair and a hand that rose to answer almost every question Mr. Steinhacker tossed out.

Malena was a science genius who could do any work given to her and answer for the rest of the class. The problem, though, was that Mr. Steinhacker knew this. He also knew his job as a teacher wasn't to teach only one student, but rather to teach *all* the students. That meant it was just a matter of time until—

"John, can you tell us the answer?"

John groaned inwardly. Mr. Steinhacker looked up from his notes, his pen pointing toward John. Malena twisted her body in her desk to stare at him. She was grinning, probably because she thought he didn't know the answer. He'd show her—that is, if he could remember the question.

"Uh, could you say that again?"

"A plant sitting in the sun will wilt. The cell structure loses water and can't support the plant's shape. What's the part of the cell that holds water and helps a plant keep its shape?"

John thought frantically, mentally searching through his memorized lists of cell parts.

"The cytoplasm?"

Malena's hand shot up instantly.

"No, not the cytoplasm," Mr. Steinhacker said, his grey eyes intense behind the rectangle frame of his glasses.

"Remember, the cytoplasm is the jelly-like liquid in the cell that allows all the other parts of the cell, the organelles, to move freely. Anyone else have an idea?"

He looked for other volunteers, trying to avoid Malena's flailing hand. None of the students offered an answer.

"Malena?"

"The vacuole keeps the plant upright. If the plant doesn't get watered enough, the plant sags like a balloon losing air."

"Exactly," Mr. Steinhacker said. As he began to discuss vacuoles more in depth, John found himself staring at the clock. Twenty-one minutes left. There were 60 seconds in a minute, so 60 times 21—John scribbled in the corner of his notebook—1,260. There were 1,260 seconds in 21 minutes, so if he counted slowly, all the way up to 1,260, he'd be able to count his way out of the class. Easy.

One. Two. Three. Four—

He sighed. It was going to be a long class.

***

After what felt like an eternity, the final bell rang. A thick mass of students flowed from the classrooms to the doors, onto the stairs, all heading towards freedom.

Instead of following them, John headed back up the stairs, pushing through the throng of students headed the other direction. His slow progress against the crowd reminded him of the photos he'd seen of salmon swimming upstream. Once he was on the fourth floor, he headed straight to Room 10. He pushed open the door, breathless. Four beaming faces stared back at him.

"John!" one of the students cried. "You made it!"

The speaker was Malena Curtina.

CHAPTER 2

"We knew you'd figure the code out," Malena said. "Now, come on!"

She grabbed John's arm and started to drag him out of the room.

"Aren't you forgetting something?" called a voice from the other end of the classroom. A boy dressed in black pants and a gray shirt sat on a desk. Black hair stuck out from beneath a black baseball cap. Everything about him was menacing. He jumped down from where he sat and made his way towards them. He was a lot shorter than John had expected. Between his height and the inviting smile spreading across his face, his ominous façade disappeared.

"Sorry, Hector," Malena said, laughing. She dropped John's arm and turned to face him. She had pretty, dark eyes that John had never noticed before. "You know who I am, right?"

"Yeah. Malena Curtina."

"Close. That's *cur-TEEN-yuh.* My dad's Jamaican, so he says you've gotta say it like that. My core is biology."

"Your 'core'?"

"My specialty. What I love to do. What I'm best at. You'll understand in a minute." Malena turned to the boy who'd spoken only a moment ago. She gave him a playful punch.

"Oww," he moaned, but he was grinning. With one hand rubbing his arm, the boy stuck out his other hand to John.

Surprised by the formality, John didn't take it at first.

"I won't bite," the boy chuckled.

John felt himself turning red, and he quickly reached for the extended hand.

"I come from Peru, and now I am friends with you," he recited with a chuckle, "I am Hector Alejandro Manuel, at your service!" the boy said, shaking it.

"Yeah," Malena cut in. "But we just call him Hector."

Hector shrugged and smiled, "Sure, that's fine too." Turning to John, he added, "Nice job figuring out the binary code."

"That was you?" John asked, surprised.

"That was me. We all created the message, and I turned it into binary. Looks like I did it right!"

"I'm Kimmey Pryce," a girl's voice cut in. "I'm in 17 percent of your classes."

A tall blonde girl stood in front of John, hand out. John recognized her instantly. She was also a regular at the front of the classroom, her hand constantly in the air. He understood in an instant why she was friends with Malena—neither of them lacked anything as far as smarts or confidence were concerned. John shook her hand as she continued talking.

"My core is physics—math, and logic," Kimmey announced. "Applied math, really. Those three make up every other form of science that's out there, so when you're busy working on your robots, just remember where your skills came from."

"Oh, come on," Malena said, rolling her eyes. "They're all important."

"Yeah. The League needs everyone," Hector said. He shot John a devilish grin. Unsure of what was going on, John rubbed his arm nervously.

"How did you know I like robots?" John asked.

Kimmey grinned. "I do my research," she said.

"We *all* do our research," Malena interjected.

"Come on, it was mostly me," Kimmey said.

"It most definitely was not!"

"Guys, guys, it doesn't matter."

John glanced over at the next speaker. She was small and dark-haired, and turning away from him to put away an *anime* book in her backpack. Up till now, John hadn't even realized she was in the room.

"I'm Natsumi Haru," the girl said. Her eyes were gentle. "I'm basically the peacekeeper here. My core is chemistry."

"Any questions?" Malena asked.

"Well, yeah," John said. The other kids laughed. "What do you guys do? What *is* this? Why am I here? I have no idea what's going on."

"You, *mi amigo,* are the newest member of the *League of Scientists*," Hector said, slapping John on the back.

"Which is?"

The kids glanced at each other.

"It's kind of like a club," Kimmey said.

"We solve mysteries," Natsumi added.

"What kind of mysteries?"

"All sorts, but mostly science. We work on mysteries that involve logic, math, chemistry, robots, physics, computers ... you know, that sort of thing. You solved one not too long ago!" Malena said.

"I did?"

"You figured out the binary code, didn't you?"

"I guess. That doesn't seem like much of a mystery, though."

"Anything's a mystery when you don't know the answer. That's what we're trying to do—find answers to the puzzles of life, or, at least, the puzzles of East Rapids!"

Natsumi laughed. "That was deep, Malena. Real deep."

"It's true, though," Malena said, turning back to John. "Anything's a mystery, really. You just have to be willing to search for the answer."

"Why do you guys solve mysteries?" John asked.

"Why not? It's fun, and we're making a difference," Kimmey answered.

"Last week," Hector said, his face serious, "we figured out who was eating all of my mom's banana chips."

"Come on, Hector! Be serious," Malena said, rolling her eyes.

Hector leaned in close to John. "It was me," he whispered.

John laughed. "Why do you guys want me, though?"

"You're the missing piece to our team," Kimmey said.

"Electronics and gadgets are really important," Malena added. "Understanding how they work and *loving* how they work—that's called passion. Passion is what built these buildings and what fills these classrooms. Passion creates. You *get* electronics, John, because you *love* electronics. The rest of us don't."

"But, Hector, didn't you write the binary code?" John asked.

"I did," said Hector, "but it sure wasn't easy. I was worried

I screwed it up and you'd go to the wrong room. I'm not confident about that sort of stuff like you. Technology is my 'core,' but programming things—that's your area, man. And robots? I don't get that stuff. You're exactly what we need."

"Really?" John said. "What do you need?"

"A new friend," Malena said, smiling.

He tried to hold back his grin so they wouldn't see just how much those words meant to him. "Why?"

"One of the things you learn growing up on an island, like Jamaica, is that friends are important, and when they can help each other out and grow together, even better. That's what the League of Scientists is all about. Jamaica is a small island, there is no other option than to be a close knit community, and I think it is something that needs to happen more in larger communities."

John felt his eyes begin to well up. Malena cut in before he could embarrass himself.

"Okay, everyone, let's get to work. Leave separately and meet up at the Lab. You guys start getting everything set up. John and I will meet you once I show him the problem. We'll take the second route in pattern *psi*. John, follow me."

Natsumi and Hector left the room and turned right. Kimmey went left, sprinting down the hall. They moved so quickly that John realized they had done this before.

He, on the other hand, was confused.

The second route in pattern "psi." What was that?

Malena grabbed John's arm and grinned. "Pick a stairwell—right, left, or straight ahead. Which way do you think we should go?"

"I have absolutely no idea."

"That's okay. How well do you know your Greek alphabet?"

"I know it starts with *alpha, beta, gamma*, and that's about it," John answered.

Malena smiled. She set her backpack down on the ground. Unzipping it, she withdrew a notebook and a pen. After making a quick drawing, she flipped the notebook around so John could see what she'd drawn.

"This is the letter *psi,* and this is the pattern we follow whenever we leave somewhere," Malena said.

The letter *psi* was shaped like a candelabra or a letter "Y" with a third vertical line splitting the top: Ψ

If Natsumi and Hector ran right and Kimmey ran left, there was one remaining "path" to take.

The middle path. Straight ahead.

"This way," John said. Malena followed him out of the classroom and toward the stairwell directly ahead, and then, always the leader, she cut in front of him. Together, they ran down the stairs and raced through the school lobby before pushing through the building's heavy green doors and heading down the street.

As they made their way toward the Lab, Malena explained to John that they'd split up for security reasons. The *psi* pattern would confuse anyone following them, hopefully breaking any pursuit before they reached the Lab. It was a lot harder to follow more than two people going separate ways than it was to follow a whole group. John laughed—*who would be following them? Why would anyone want to hurt them?*

CHAPTER 3

John hurried to keep up with Malena, dodging awkwardly around the wide green bushes planted around the school.

Malena headed toward the business district, leading John past small shops and restaurants. She slowed her pace when she noticed him struggling to keep up.

"We're almost there," she encouraged.

"Good." John said, panting heavily.

Malena glanced back, the purple beads in her braids clicking together as she did so. "Coast is clear. I don't think we're being followed anymore," she said with a sigh of relief.

"What?" John exclaimed, spinning around. He expected to see someone lurking suspiciously behind them.

Malena burst out laughing. Realizing she was just kidding, John shook his head reproachfully at her.

"You know, you might get into trouble for that one day. Someone's not going to believe you when you really need them to."

"Hey, when I'm serious, you'll know. I promise."

They walked awhile in companionable silence when Malena abruptly said, "Over here, you have to see something. The others are setting up at the Lab, but you need to check this out."

John looked at her curiously. She wasn't smiling anymore.

They walked down Orchard View, one of the more popular streets in town, especially for the students at East Rapids. A lot of cool hangouts within biking distance made the town great for kids. It had everything John loved: cheap food, a library, and a game store.

They cut through a parking lot, weaving between parked cars to get to the crosswalk. After walking a bit more, Malena held up a hand.

"Stop."

John looked at the building in front of them, confused.

"Krazy Carly's?"

"No," Malena said. "We can get hot dogs later."

She took John's arm and spun him away from the café. Directly in front of them was an elegant metal streetlight. Standing about ten feet tall, it was coated in several layers of shiny black paint.

"Notice anything about the light?" she asked.

John peered up at it expectantly before he gave a reply.

"Yeah. The shards of glass sticking out of the socket. Looks like the bulb is broken."

"Right. But look at that thick protective glass. You've got to remove those four panels if you want to get to the light bulb, right? Replacing a burned-out bulb is a pain."

"So?" John huffed. "What's the point? Why are you showing me this?"

"This is *my* city too, John. My home. *Our home.* And that streetlight belongs to all of us."

Malena's dark eyes glared up at the shattered bulb. "We don't like someone hurting our community, and neither does the rest of the League. We solve mysteries because it's fun and challenging, but there's another reason. We want to make East Rapids a better place. This is our community and we need to make sure it is a good place. We have to find out who did this."

"But how do you know that a person broke this light bulb? Maybe it shattered in a storm. Or the bulbs are faulty. There's also the possibility that there is a short circuit in the wiring."

"My aunt is a sergeant for the police department. That's how I found out about this. The bulb keeps breaking somehow, but the protective glass is never removed or broken. The only thing that's busted is the bulb inside. They've checked out the light and they know it's not an electrical problem. It's got to be a person. The owner of Krazy Carly's keeps reporting it. The city keeps replacing the bulb, but within a few days it's broken again. No one ever sees the crime, but it keeps happening."

"Breaking the bulb without damaging the protective glass—how do you do that?"

"Exactly. How? That's the mystery we've got to solve. After we solve that, maybe we can find out when and why this keeps happening."

"And who did it!"

"You've got it. That's the reason why we need your help, John. Help us solve this mystery."

"What? Right now?"

"Yes, now. Let's head to the Lab and talk to the League."

Malena's eyes were still flashing from her passionate speech, but there was also a smile on her face now. Malena had some kind of inner strength or charisma. Whatever it was, she used it to lead the group.

Then John was once again sprinting, trying to keep up.

***

The Lab was an old shed tucked in the corner of Kimmey's backyard. It had been given a fresh set of white paint to match the house, making it bright against the row of dark trees marking the boundary of the Pryce property. Just a few feet beyond the property line, the ground gave way to a ravine with the remnants of a small stream at the bottom. The smell of decaying plants and fresh water floated by on a breeze while the sound of crickets and frogs filled the air with noise.

John followed Malena into the shed and then paused to let his eyes adjust to the lighting. The inside had been redone as well—the floor was wooden, and the walls were painted a cheerful yellow. A large photograph hung in the center of the shed between two windows. It was of Malena, Kimmey, Natsumi, and Hector, taken about a year ago. They were standing in front of an ice cream shop, arms around each other, laughing. Looking at the photograph, he suddenly felt very lonely. He couldn't help but think that he didn't belong there. They already had each other; he was a fifth wheel.

That seemed so long ago but John could still remember every detail.

"What do you think?" Malena asked.

"It's cool," he answered. He let his eyes skip across the room, falling on Hector and Natsumi laughing together at the small round table near the door. Near them, Kimmey sat at a small desk, her face only inches away from a laptop screen. "How long has the League existed?"

"We formed the club last year when we all started middle school," Malena answered. "Kimmey, Natsumi, and I became friends in science class. Then I had a math class with Hector, and he was such a weirdo that we just had to adopt him."

Hector's head spun toward Malena. "Hey!" he called with mock indignation. "I am not a weirdo!"

Malena laughed. "You were always messing with the teacher's computer!"

Hector grinned mischievously. "So?"

Malena turned back to John, smiling. "We all just started hanging out together. We solved one mystery, and then another, and in no time we made it official by giving it a name. I don't really know how these things happen. They just do."

"Are you guys done talking yet?" Kimmey asked. She sounded almost annoyed.

"What's your problem?" Hector snapped.

She looked away from the computer screen, surprised. "I wasn't trying to be rude, but we do have a mystery to solve here."

"I already tried to set up a video feed," Hector said, "but I don't have anything with a battery life long enough to leave out all night. The bulb-breaking seems to happen overnight and always after Krazy Carly's shuts down. That's at 6:00 p.m. This time of year, it's dark by 5:30 p.m."

"There are four conditions, then," Kimmey said. She put her elbow on the table and lifted a thin finger. "One, we can't record a video to find the bad guy."

"Or girl," Hector interjected. "Why does everyone always assume the bad guy is a guy?"

"Or girl," Kimmey said, rolling her eyes.

"We don't even know that it's a person," Natsumi added.

"What else could it be?" Kimmey asked.

"I don't know," Natsumi admitted, "but isn't part of being a good scientist not jumping to conclusions?"

Kimmey sighed. “You’re right. So whatever is happening, we can’t use video to catch him, her, or it.”

“Next condition,” she continued, lifting a second finger. “It seems to happen at night. We all have to be home by 10:00 p.m. so staying out all night and staring at a streetlight isn’t an option. Even if we could, it doesn’t seem to happen *every* night. It’s only once in a while.

“Third,” she brought three fingers together and grabbed them with her other hand. “Whatever happens, happens fast. No one has seen it being done.”

“Fourth, it breaks the streetlight bulb without breaking the protective glass around the outside. Those are the facts, and that is all we know with certainty. Simple.”

“Simple?” John said. “How is that simple?”

Kimmey grinned. “Well, the *facts* are simple. The solution isn’t. That’s why you’re here, Mr. Expert.”

“Great,” John said. “I’m glad there’s no pressure.”

Natsumi leaned forward in her chair.

“We haven’t found an answer yet, John, but there is one. There always is.” She paused and grinned.

Natsumi empathized with John. She knew how hard challenges seemed at the beginning. *It was always good to break a problem down into pieces. Then you could solve each piece one at a time. Kimmey was good at reminding them to do that.*

Encouraged by Natsumi’s empathy, John began to think. If they couldn’t make a video, that was fine. They could collect other kinds of data. His robot kits at home had tons of tiny battery-powered devices for measuring light, humidity, vibration, sound, and plenty of other properties. John knew that measuring data was critical for good science. Ask any volcanologist: How do you predict a volcanic eruption when all triggers of that eruption are going on inside the earth? By measuring data.

"No pressure...," John sighed nervously. He squinted, thinking hard.

"*Calmate*, everyone, hold it," Hector said, pretending to push away the rest of the League. "Nobody breathe! Let John's brain get all the oxygen!" The others laughed.

John blushed and smiled as he thought some more. What kind of data would let you know when the bulb broke? How could you figure that out? And still the mystery remained: Why was the inside bulb broken when the outside glass wasn't?

John slowly lifted his head and looked around. Kimmey was staring at him hard, her head cocked to the side. Malena's eyes were comically wide and expectant. Natsumi had sat back again and gave John an encouraging smile when she caught him glancing at her. John returned the smile, but then suddenly frowned in concentration.

Hector grinned and said, "You've figured it out, haven't you?"

John grinned back. "Maybe. I don't know who's doing it or why. But I think we can figure out when the bulb breaks, and we don't need a video camera."

Malena nodded her head in affirmation. "Cool. I knew we needed you in the League."

John took a few more minutes to think through his plan and then he took in a deep breath before addressing his audience.

"Okay," John said. "First, I have to thank someone." He turned to Natsumi. "*Arigato,* Natsumi. Is that the right Japanese word?"

"Well, yes," Natsumi said, and her voice rose with her eyebrows. "*Dou itashimashite.* You're welcome. But why? What did I do?"

"You gave me the idea about pressure. That's the key to finding out when the bulb breaks. I can make a special pressure monitor for the streetlight. Or in this case, a vibration monitor. I don't care if the culprit is a daylight-fearing, glass-eating, flying elf. Anyone breaking that bulb just *has* to be touching the streetlight—shaking it, moving it, climbing it, whatever. So we set up a vibration monitor. It can run for days on one battery. It doesn't need light to 'see' what's happening. And it's small, so no one will notice it."

"Like a scientist waiting for a volcano to erupt," Malena murmured in sudden understanding. "The scientist doesn't watch the volcano itself; instead they monitor vibrations and pressure around the volcano!"

"Don't forget to name it!" Hector insisted.

"What?" John asked, confused.

"Your monitor. Any time you make something, *always* give it a name. You made it, right? So, you need to name it."

"I think he means it's your baby, in a way," Malena translated for Hector. "Your creation."

"Um, okay," John said without conviction. He never named his creations, but one look at Hector's intense expression changed his mind about this one.

"I'll name it," John quickly assured Hector. "But first, we have to install it, right? I'll set up the monitor and wait for the bulb to break. Then we can look at the monitor, check the vibrations from the previous night, and see what time the biggest vibration occurred. The biggest vibration should mark the moment the bulb broke. Then we set it up again and wait for another break, to make sure the data match up."

"That sounds perfect," Kimmey said. "You get me three or four exact times, and I'll find a pattern. Then we'll know when the next break will happen."

“What do we do when we know the timing of the next break?” John asked.

The answer was obvious. Everyone answered in unison.

“We’ll be there!”

CHAPTER 4

It was three weeks later when the League gathered again on a bright and brisk afternoon. “I’ve got good news and more good news,” John announced. He was at the Lab with his new friends. They were all sitting around a big table with a small pile of electronics in front of them.

Malena laughed. “Oh, no. Better tell us the *good* news first.”

“Hold on, John,” Hector said, staring at the pile. “The more important thing: Did you name it?”

“Uh, no,” John said. “Sorry. I forgot.”

Hector shook his head in mock disappointment. “Then your news better be really, really good.”

"I think it is. I messed up at first, though. I used an old battery, and that died on me pretty quick. But I went back and fixed it, and still got a few days' worth of good data."

"Awesome," Kimmey said. "You've got times and dates for us?"

"Yeah, a few. Just over twenty thousand."

Kimmey's mouth dropped open, and the group was silent until Malena spoke up.

"There's got to be something wrong."

"That's what I thought," John said. "I figured I attached the vibration monitor wrong or the electronics freaked out on me. So I tested it the best way I knew: I sat down next to the streetlight, plugged my laptop into the monitor and watched in real time. The vibrations are legit. Guess what they are?"

"Earthquakes," guessed Hector.

"Maybe lightning," suggested Kimmey.

"Cars," Natsumi said.

John looked at her, surprised. "Natsumi's right!"

Hector smacked his head then fixed his hat. "Cars. Of course. The streetlight is—what—five feet away from traffic? It shakes every time a car drives past."

"Right," John said. "That's part one of the good news: the monitor works really well. Part two comes when we look at the data. The car traffic is only a bunch of little shakes, really tiny vibrations, compared to some really massive hits."

"You better tell me," said Kimmey, "that you've got fewer than twenty thousand massive hits."

"Yeah. I've got three."

The group was silent for a moment.

"Perfect," Malena whispered.

"The three big hits to the streetlight happened every Monday for the last three weeks. It didn't even matter if the bulb was already broken or not. They all happened sometime after 9:00 p.m."

"That's simple," said Kimmey, shrugging. "Next time, give me a real problem."

"Simple?" said Hector. "Then, you're smarter than I am. I sure don't get it."

"Look at the pattern. We've got three hits. They happen every Monday just after 9:00 p.m.."

"So?"

"So, what do you think happens every Monday night and finishes up a little before 9:00 p.m.?"

Hector looked perplexed. "I don't know, Krazy Carly's has a dollar menu? The library closes? Oh wait, I know, salsa dancing at the community center finishes!"

Kimmey sighed. "Hector, you're not on the basketball team, are you?

"Well, no, I like watching basketball, and sometimes ***fútbol,*** but I don't really play any sports, especially since I'm about a foot shorter than most of the players. My sport is video games."

"That's not a sport," Kimmey said, rolling her eyes. "Sports have to get you sweaty."

"I get sweaty when I play video games!"

"Eww!"

"Wait a minute," Natsumi said. Her eyes were suddenly intense. "My brother is on the basketball team. Varsity basketball practice is Monday, Wednesday, and Friday. It ends at 7:00 p.m. But Monday nights they stay later, though, and have a sort of team pep rally. That ends around 8:30 p.m."

"Exactly," Kimmey said, nodding.

Malena's eyes lit up. "Okay, let's focus on the basketball team. Who else do we know on the team? Who on the team walks home from school? That's easy enough to figure out—"

"Dowser," John blurted out. "Dowser's on the basketball team. I don't know where he lives, but I know he walks home."

The more John thought about it, the more it made perfect sense.

"Who's Dowser?" Natsumi asked. Their school was pretty big, but that name was unique enough to stand out.

"Brandon LaMange," John answered. "He's a bully. I just call him Dowser because he's kind of clueless, you know? Like, he just skirts through life, looking for someone else to set him on his next path—mainly, who to pick on next. Like someone dowsing for water with dowsing rods."

John stopped talking when he noticed everyone watching him in silence. It was a little uncomfortable, like they were analyzing him. He thought about what he should say next, cleared his throat, and then he spoke again.

"It's got to be Dowser. He's always been a jerk. He doesn't care about anyone else. He'll push me into a wall just so he can watch me fall down. He's probably breaking the light for the fun of it."

Natsumi frowned. "I'm sorry, John. He's in a few of my classes, too. He *is* a jerk. But you can't just assume—"

"In fact," John interrupted, "I'll bet he *does* live around here. It'd be easy to tell. We could see if his family's address is listed in the school directory. Or … or we follow him home. We'd need to split up, though, so he doesn't see all of us following him. We could stay at a distance on our bikes."

"Or," Hector said, "we just look up his address online." Hector pulled a laptop out of his backpack. He opened it, balanced it on his knees, and started typing. "Okay, what's his last name? 'LaMange,' right?"

John nodded. Kimmey shoved forward to watch as Hector typed and clicked.

Hector looked up. "We've got three LaMange families in East Rapids."

"Let's see," Kimmey said while motioning for Hector to do just that.

Hector turned the laptop around to face the rest of the group. The screen showed a map of East Rapids with three red dots marking different locations.

"Look!" Kimmey said with excitement. She snatched Hector's laptop and plopped it on the table, closer to the rest of the group. Hector squinted in pain as they handled his new computer.

"Here and here," she poked hard at the screen. The laptop wobbled and Hector winced again. "These two houses are in the wrong direction. There's only one house near the streetlight. Even then, you'd be going out of your way to walk past the streetlight."

"So, Dowser cuts by the streetlight on his way home from practice," John mused, thinking hard. "He stops to shatter the light bulb and then he goes home," he concluded.

"Are you serious?"Kimmey said, her eyebrows rose.

"Yeah! I really think it's him!"

"Wait a minute. We can't just assume it's Dowser—I mean Brandon—just because he's not the nicest person in the world."

"Dowser doesn't care about anyone or anything. He likes to hit anything that's available. He's the perfect suspect."

"John," Natsumi spoke quietly. "Kimmey isn't fighting you. She's looking at the situation logically."

"So am I! It makes perfect sense!"

"John, no. You're investigating this the wrong way. Use the scientific process."

"I'm not guessing! There might be plenty of reasons why Dowser would break the light. And anyway, since when does he need a reason? He's been picking on me ever since I got here for no real reason."

"The scientific process means you collect evidence and then analyze it to see if it supports your prediction."

"That's what I'm doing!"

Natsumi shook her head.

"No. You gathered data, and that's good. But then you got focused on Dowser and tried to find reasons why he'd break the light. Anyone can come up with reasons to believe whatever they want, and that's what you're doing. You have an idea, so you're looking for ways to support it. That's the opposite of what a real scientist does. A real scientist looks at the data and *that* leads to the answer. The answer is always *after* the data. Never before."

Malena tipped back her chair and bit into an orange slice, quiet except for the chair's metallic creak. Even so, her manner had changed. John and Kimmey paused and looked at her. Malena looked at Hector's laptop.

"We're missing something else," she declared.

She slammed her chair back down to the floor, grabbed Hector's laptop and held it up, showing the screen to the group.

"Hey, *cuidado!*" Hector said, "you're really not supposed to hold it by the screen like that."

"Sorry," Malena said. "But I'm making a point: See what day it is? Anyone notice the time?"

She pointed to the clock and calendar displayed on Hector's laptop. It read, "*Monday, 19:11.*"

"Nineteen?" Natsumi said. "What time is that?"

"Time for a new clock," Kimmey joked.

"No," Hector replied. "It's military time. They use a 24-hour clock to avoid any confusion. All you have to do is subtract twelve hours if the time is after noon. So, when you see

19:00, that means 7:00 p.m. Right now, it's 7:11, and ... oh! It's Monday. That means that tonight is the night!"

"I passed the streetlight on my way to school this morning," Malena said slowly, trying to remember. "They were putting in a new bulb. We're less than two hours from another break. I say we meet here in an hour. Then we'll visit the streetlight. We can see if anyone else is there."

Malena looked at John.

"You did great, John, getting us this data. Now that we have a hypothesis for when the light breaks, let's watch what happens, and we'll see if we're right."

CHAPTER 5

An hour later, the five friends met up at the new solar fountain in the town square, a block away from Krazy Carly's. The benches surrounding the fountain formed an oblong shape. Though it was nice weather for early December most of the benches were empty. Despite the few streetlights surrounding them, it was very dark outside.

They all dressed in black, wanting to blend into their surroundings. They copied the look of the folks who change sets in the theatre between scenes. Unlike the stage hands, John realized, out here in public, their outfits actually made them stand out. The uniform black appearance made them look menacing.

They were not anticipating an audience to be there to watch them, but there was nothing they could do about it. As the kids congregated around an empty bench to prepare a plan of action, the people in the park watched them warily, especially as Hector began pulling things out of his equally dark backpack. Noticing the public stares, Kimmey offered a cheerful wave to put them at ease, but it only came off as insolent. The people around them began to leave. Kimmey shrugged her shoulders, turning back to the group.

"Always have the right tool for the job, soldier," Hector said as he pulled two walkie-talkies out of his backpack and handed them to John. Then, focusing once more on his backpack, Hector pulled out a camera. He handed it to Malena. "This doesn't have night vision, but we should be able to record enough by the streetlamp's light—at least until it's broken."

Kimmey plucked one walkie-talkie from John's hand.

"I'll take one of these and go with John. You guys take the other one and take the camera too since you've got an extra person."

"Fine," Malena said. "You two stay here and blend in with the bushes or something. Whoever it is breaking the bulb won't notice you that way. Radio us when someone's coming, and my team will hide close to the streetlight so we can get a video—somewhere like the outside wall of Krazy Carly's. Hector, you take the camera since you know how to use it best. Natsumi, you take the other walkie-talkie."

"And you?" Natsumi asked. There was a short burst of static as she turned on the walkie-talkie.

"I'll watch the fun." Malena gave a quirky smile.

As the group disappeared to their various assignments, John and Kimmey left their spot on the bench and moved closer to the fountain. Thick, wobbling streams of water shot from one end of the fountain to the other. There were so many arcs of water that the entire fountain seemed to shimmer. They stayed on the far side of the fountain to hide in the water's shadow. If anyone were to look directly at them, the arcing water would distort whatever was left of them to see.

John and Kimmey couldn't see the streetlight from their position, but they could see the middle school gym.

Basketball practice let out, and students spilled from the gym's doors, running, walking, skating and biking away. John saw Dowser. He was walking with a boy he didn't know. They each had a basketball and were showing off dribbling tricks as they walked slowly down the street.

" Okay," Kimmey spoke into the walkie-talkie. "Basketball practice is done. There's a bunch of people heading your way now. We see Dowser."

"Okay. We're in position," Natsumi's voice crackled.

Kimmey sat down on the concrete edge of the fountain to wait. One of her legs jiggled impatiently. John paced back and forth, stopping periodically to look at the walkie-talkie. Both of them jumped when the device spoke.

"Guys, here comes someone," Natsumi whispered, and her transmitted voice sounded sinister. "Hector has got the camera on the streetlight. Malena's watching the students."

There was a pause. John hurried to sit down beside Kimmey.

"It's 9:10. Someone's got to do it. Real soon."

John and Kimmey heard what happened next through the walkie-talkie.

There was a loud thump then a tinkle of broken glass. Someone laughing. A boy. Eyes wide, Kimmey and John looked at each other. They both leaned closer to the walkie-talkie.

"Got him." Now it was Malena's voice. "It wasn't Dowser. It was the guy with him. I don't know who he is."

Kimmey looked over at John. He tried not to let his disappointment show. He'd really wanted it to be Dowser. He'd thought that maybe if the humiliation of getting caught was high enough, Dowser would understand what it was like to be pointed out and shamed. He thought maybe Dowser would leave him alone then. But no. The bullying would continue.

***

The League met back at the Lab. Hector fiddled with his camera for a few moments. Then he pulled out his laptop, set it on the table and rotated it toward the group. The laptop screen displayed a close up view of someone's nostrils.

"That's me. I was just making sure the camera worked."

"Well, it did," Kimmey said, wrinkling her nose in disgust. "Can we stop looking up your nose now?"

"Right. Just a second."

Hector pushed a button on the camera and the video jumped ahead at twice the normal speed. The laptop showed a high-speed pan to his feet, then a brick wall, then a small alley between buildings. It finally zeroed in on the streetlight. The image jerked and shuddered rapidly as Hector adjusted focus and position. Students began to walk by the streetlight, coming into momentary view as they emerged beneath the streetlight and disappearing just as quickly as they walked away. Their legs moved impossibly fast and their arms gestured with snake-like speed.

"Here we go," Hector said, watching the playback timer. "Back to normal speed."

He pushed a button on the camera. The video speed slowed to real time. The sound came back too, and the laptop spoke in Natsumi's voice.

"Guys, here comes someone. Hector's got the camera on the streetlight. Malena's watching the students."

John barely heard the rest of the audio. He stared at the screen, waiting. He felt his heart beating. Even though he'd heard what happened, Malena hadn't solved the mystery, insisting they find out together how the streetlight was broken.

A few more students filtered by, voices and laughter mixing into an audio blur. Then John heard a new noise, a slow *thump ... thump ... thump.* It grew louder. A student came into view, dribbling a basketball from hand to hand. It was the kid who had walked with Dowser.

But Dowser was nowhere to be seen. The boy was alone.

He casually looked up and down the square, then across the street. He lifted the basketball. Throwing with both hands from his chest, he flung the ball toward the streetlight.

He had good aim. John watched, shocked, as the ball slammed into the upper half of the streetlight just under the light fixture. The blow shattered the fragile glass bulb inside. The thicker, protective glass around it was undamaged.

Hector paused the video, leaving the broken streetlight frozen on the screen.

"He hit the pole with a basketball!" John said. "It was that easy!"

"Who is this kid, anyway?" Hector asked.

"I don't know," Malena said. "I don't care. We don't need his name."

"Why not?"

"Because it won't happen again."

"What? How do you know?" Hector asked.

Malena didn't answer. Her eyes narrowed in determination.

"Oh, I know that look!" Kimmey said. "You're going to do something sneaky, aren't you?"

Malena slowly grinned.

***

The next morning, students were shoving their way into their classrooms just as the last bell chimed. The voice on the corner-mounted TV was reciting the usual student-produced school news: sports report, cafeteria menu, and special announcements. John had arrived early and was already sitting and watching.

At the final segment, the feed changed from text slides to video. The "ERMS News Desk" was really a cafeteria table shoved against a blank wall of the video production lab. Brad Webber sat on a chair, forearms resting on the table. His hair was carefully combed, and then combed again. He took the job of reporting very seriously.

"We've got something different today," Brad read from a notepad, excitedly. "A group calling themselves, 'The League of Scientists,' has sent us a video. They've solved a local mystery and want to keep it from happening again."

The video from Hector's camera was suddenly on the screen. There was an image of the boy walking up to the streetlight, but now his face was pixelated. John realized Malena must have had Hector electronically hide the boy's face.

The video showed the basketball arcing to hit the streetlamp. As the ball reached its destination, the glowing bulb suddenly went dark and the faint sounds of the shards hitting the protective covering echoed.

"This is vandalism. The principal will be speaking with this student to ensure that this does not happen again. To the rest of East Rapids Middle School, a warning: if it's not yours, don't mess with it. If this happens again, the police will get involved. Respect your community and respect each other!" Brad finished, his brows furrowing for emphasis.

John smiled to himself. Dowser's friend wouldn't be committing vandalism anymore, not after being exposed like that, with or without a pixelated face. He only wished it had been Dowser.

He looked away from the TV and froze.

Dowser was staring right at him. His eyes burning angrily, John almost expected to smell smoke.

He thinks I'm the one who videotaped his friend.

John hunched over his notebook and pretended to take notes. Anything to turn his face away from Dowser because the red flush crawling up his neck would certainly give him away. Even though John hadn't filmed the video or submitted it to the school, he'd been involved nevertheless. And Dowser knew it.

***

John walked into Ms. Heida's class and smiled at Kimmey before he sat down behind her. He couldn't imagine that he would have ever become friends with her if it hadn't been for the League. As Ms. Heida started telling the class about the ancient Greeks, John let his mind wander.

Yes, he thought, *the League of Scientists had set his life on a new path.*

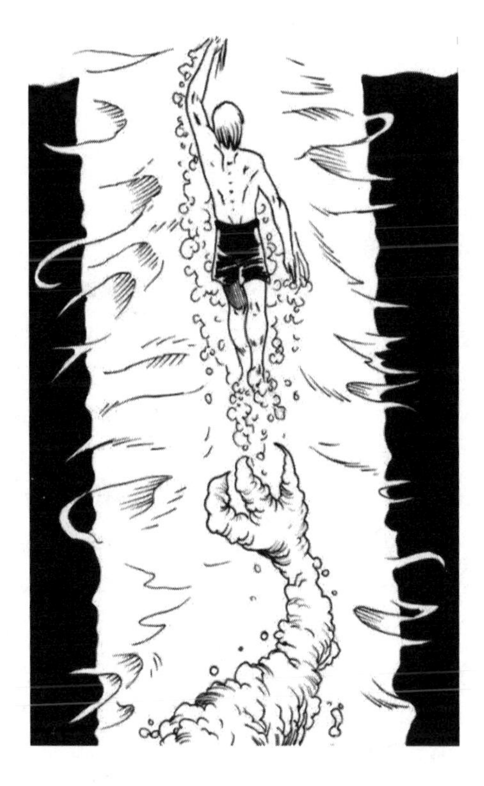

CHAPTER 6

Casey Keller dove into the pool. He somersaulted underwater, slapped the bottom with both feet and rocketed back up. Surfacing, the pungent smell of chlorine filled his nostrils as he breathed in deeply. He loved that smell. He was where he wanted to be, doing what he enjoyed.

This was his favorite time of day—early morning, long before the other students arrived, before most of them were even awake. He hadn't seen Coach Warren and would leap out of the pool if he came by. Casey wasn't supposed to be swimming alone; it was against school policy after all. But

Casey had been swimming since he was in diapers and loved the freedom and feel of the water.

Time to practice. The swim team needed it. The team needed *him* this year more than ever. Casey thought of some of the newer swimmers and sighed. It just meant that he'd have to do that much better on next week during the swim meet against West Shore. It was only five days away!

Warmed up, he began a fast freestyle, cutting through the water like a speedboat. He stayed in the second lane near the wall. In competitions, he would dust everyone else from the center lane, but when he practiced alone, it made sense to stick near the edge in case he cramped.

His heart rate and breathing were steady as he sped through the water. He did a flip-turn and zoomed back down the lane.

A sudden chill was the first indication to Casey that something was wrong. The pool air was colder than usual. The early morning sun was just peeking in through the massive windows of the indoor pool, so the pool's greenhouse effect hadn't had a chance to kick in yet.

At first, the water was fine, but as he swam, he'd pass through a chilly spot every once in a while. Not just chilly, he corrected himself, but freezing. *What was this? Was the pool's heat pump malfunctioning?*

As he slowed down his laps, Casey noticed something occurring near the pool's edge. It was hard to focus through the fog of his goggles. Pulling them off, he realized the fog was not on his goggles—it was in the room. A layer of fog hung over the pool. A gentle cloud curled, twisted, and brushed the surface of the water. It began moving toward him. Perplexed at the scene unfolding around him, he had no idea what was going on. Casey kept treading water as he stared at the cloud accumulating in mass. It moved quickly until it was now directly in front of him—only a few feet from his face. Casey looked into the

swirling fog and thought he saw something familiar. He squinted and leaned closer trying to decipher the outline.

It grew colder still, and Casey felt his muscles stiffening from the lack of heat. His teeth chattered and goose bumps pierced through the skin on his arms and legs. It became harder to tread water.

This isn't real, Casey thought. It was too strange to be real, and yet there he was, watching and feeling it. This wasn't a dream. He had to get out *now*!

Sometimes, a person sees things that bring their animal instincts front and center. All worries are forgotten and all problems disappear except for survival. The logical part of Casey's brain shut down in terror. His animal instincts took over. His basic instincts told him to get away, to escape.

Choking and spluttering, Gripped by fear, Casey tried to swim for the opposite side of the pool, away from the cold water, away from the fog. His strokes were wild; finesse meant nothing now. His movements were inefficient and choppy as though he'd only just learned how to swim. Arms moved only to push him away from the danger and legs kicked without rhythm. His breath came in raspy and fast and he choked on a mouthful of water. He could barely hold back a panicked cry.

Then, only feet from the pool's edge, he made a mistake. He looked back. He saw a hand. A gelatinous tentacle. A stretching claw.

He saw a ghost!

It shot towards him from beneath the water. Moving fast, it reached toward his legs. It glowed a sickly dark orange, opening its claws as if to grab him.

Casey thought he felt a claw reach his ankle. He shrieked. These sounds also came from the primal animal within—the fleeing prey. High piercing sobs punctuated his frantic splashes. His kicking and punching at the water moved him slowly to the other edge of the pool. The gigantic, empty room amplified his cries.

He grabbed the side of the pool. Scrambling and grappling his way over the edge carelessly, Casey's skin was scraped off his elbows, stomach, and knees, but he didn't even feel it. He stumbled up on weak, shaking legs. Water spattered onto the floor as his feet flailed wildly running to the locker room.

He took a last look at the pool right before he ran under the doorframe. He could no longer see the glowing orange of the ghostlike thing that made a grab for him. The pool shone an eerie ghostly green. Casey quickly slammed the door and dragged the laundry cart to barricade himself inside.

Gasping for breath, he swore he'd never go back into that pool *ever* again.

CHAPTER 7

"Did you hear about Casey Keller?"

John and Malena sat in Mr. Steinhacker's science class. Malena still sat in the front row and John, wanting to sit near his friend, slouched in the seat behind her. He felt exposed being so close to the front of the class. John wiggled with agitation in his seat, trying to make himself one with the chair, but then abruptly stopped. He was sure that everyone was now staring at him. He sank even further down in his seat and felt his face grow warm. *Why couldn't Malena sit in the back of the class?*

Malena didn't mind attention. It almost seemed like she wanted to draw attention to herself. John scowled at the uncomfortable thought. She had her hand up for almost every question Mr. Steinhacker asked.

When Malena wasn't answering questions, she was talking to John, which he enjoyed… just not during Mr. Steinhacker's lecture.

"I heard. He told me himself," John said, sliding even lower, trying to keep his voice as quiet as possible.

"What? I can't hear you."

"I said, I heard. Casey told me."

"Me, too. He's told everyone twice by now!"

"Let's talk later. Steinhacker's watching."

Malena glanced at their teacher. He hadn't even noticed them; he was too caught up in the science he loved.

"The anglerfish," Mr. Steinhacker continued deep into his lecture, "is a perfect example of mutualism."

He gestured with a remote, and the image on the projector screen slid aside to reveal a truly nasty-looking fish.

"See the long, thin, sharp teeth? This upward-pointing shovel of a mouth? Look at this little ball of light, hanging from the forehead. Look how it glows! Can anyone tell me *how* it glows?"

"He doesn't care," Malena whispered to John from the corner of her mouth as she raised her hand to answer. "We're fine."

John shifted uncomfortably. He didn't like talking in class. He was afraid that he'd either be yelled at or that he would get called on and answer a question incorrectly. He didn't want his classmate's or the teacher's eyes on him or their judgment.

Mr. Steinhacker listened to another student then kindly responded.

"Actually, it's not from the fish itself. The little ball glows because of bacteria. The fish and the bacteria have a symbiotic relationship. The glowing bacteria help the anglerfish attract food. In return, they get a nice place to live. This mutual partnership is different from other symbiotic relationships such as parasitism and commensalism. In a symbiotic relationship, there is at least one organism dependent on another but in predation and competition, the organisms are only dependent on themselves."

The screen image slid aside again, now showing the anglerfish from a distance. It was hard to see—the fish was almost black, except for its pencil thin, knife-edged teeth and the glowing lure dangling above its skeletal face.

Malena turned around completely in her chair to face John.

"Hey!" she whispered, a little too loudly, "Maybe that's it!"

"What's it?"

"The ghost in the water. Could it be some kind of glowing bacteria?"

"I don't know," John mumbled, keeping his voice low. "Can we talk about this later? I don't want to get in trouble."

"What?" Malena whispered loudly. "I can't hear you."

Mr. Steinhacker, suddenly in front of them, knocked on Malena's table. John jumped. Malena wrinkled her nose and turned slowly back around.

"Malena, John said he'd like to talk about this later. I think that's a good idea."

"Okay," she said, swiveling her head to look briefly at John. The beads at the end of her braids clicked together as she flashed John a knowing smile. Then she turned back around, flipping open her notebook as she did so. As Mr. Steinhacker resumed his lecture, Malena began scribbling. To John, it looked like she was taking notes.

After a couple of minutes though, she stopped writing and slowly, quietly tore a page from her notebook. Turning ever so slightly, she flicked the paper onto John's table and then turned back. It happened so fast, John didn't have time to react. He just stared at the paper. It read:

After School, Before Home
Mouse eats elephant's tusk.
Anglerfish's teeth.
The hadopelagic environment, lives amphipods bacteria.

This was no note; it was a puzzle. The first line was simple enough: Malena wanted to meet up with him after school ended before they left for home, but what did the other sentences mean? They were filled with biology references, Malena's core, but the science, despite Malena's intelligence, was shaky. Even John knew that. *Mice eating tusks?* His brain began to hurt from trying to figure out what she meant. He usually dealt with non-living, non-judgmental, inhuman batteries and wires.

He didn't know what mice or tusks had to do with anything, and anglerfish teeth were an unpleasant thought. The only part of the puzzle that made any sense to him was the last part, about the bacteria. Malena seemed to be hinting at the ghost Casey claimed to have seen in the pool. Mr. Steinhacker had just said bacteria could glow. What if someone had filled the pool with bacteria and *that* was what Casey saw?

John focused on the previous two lines. He read them over and over again, lingering over words, parts of words, and individual letters. His pen measured his progress as he pointed it at each word. He bit the inside of his cheek and furrowed his brows.

He wasn't very good at cryptology, but it couldn't be that hard. He said each sentence backwards. He tried switching the first letters of each pair of words. He checked to see if the individual words made sense if you read them backwards. He underlined the first letter of each word.

After School, Before Home

Mouse eats elephant's tusk.

Anglerfish's teeth.

The hadopelagic environment, lives amphipods bacteria.

Bingo! He figured it out!

Right after school before he went home, Malena wanted to "*Meet At The Lab.*"

John took a deep breath and gathered his courage, trying to forget about the many students behind him. After Mr. Steinhacker turned away from the class to write on the whiteboard, John leaned forward.

"I'll be there."

He sat back quickly, sure that Mr. Steinhacker would see him.

Malena turned her head slightly to the side and nodded. Then she raised her hand to answer the next question.

***

"No," said Malena. "It couldn't have been bacteria."

Back at the Lab, the League clustered around their table to discuss the mystery. Hector's face was a shade paler from the glow of his laptop screen. His fingers were poised to type the League's next big plan to unravel the ghost in the water mystery. So far, they didn't have much.

Malena continued with her deductions. "After Casey ran out to get help, teachers came back and tested the water. They didn't find anything. The water looked normal—no glow. Bacteria wouldn't just disappear like that. There would be something left behind. Besides, it takes a *lot* of bacteria to make a little light. Bacteria lighting up the whole pool? I don't think that's even possible. You couldn't dump huge quantities of bacteria in a pool and then make it all disappear so quickly."

Natsumi thought for a moment. "You're right. Besides, the chlorine in the pool would kill the bacteria. That's the reason it's there!"

"But it *did* happen," John insisted. "Casey said so."

Kimmey flicked her blue eyes over to John. "Casey's probably lying," she sighed.

"Why would he lie?" John asked, suddenly nervous beneath Kimmey's intense stare. Though John liked her, their friendship was still too new for him to feel completely comfortable around her.

"I don't know," Kimmey mused. "Let's just say for a minute that the glowing pool scenario isn't possible—that it didn't happen. Instead of a ghost, Casey could have . . ."

"I'm only saying the hypothesis about bacteria is probably wrong, not that the pool didn't glow," Malena interrupted Kimmey's train of thought. "What Casey saw still could've happened."

"How?" Kimmey asked incredulously.

"We don't know," Malena admitted. She sat back, looking thoughtful. "We don't know *yet*, but we'll figure it out. I don't think Casey's lying. He was scared. You guys know what a good swimmer he is. Now he says he doesn't want to go back into the pool!"

"There's a big swim meet on Tuesday," Hector interjected. "That's only four days away! It's against West Shore and Casey's our star swimmer. He'd better get back in the water or the team is dead on arrival!"

Kimmey turned to look at him in shock.

"You said you didn't like sports!"

Hector shrugged. "People talk. I listen."

"That's a good skill to have," Malena noted. "Listening to other people talk gives us some good data. Let's list what we know. Hector, can you take notes?"

"Why?"

"So we won't forget anything. If we solve this mystery, we can post it online or something. That's good advertising for the League of Scientists. We'll need to show what we can do before people will take us seriously."

"What people?" John asked.

"Everyone. Kids. Adults."

"You think an adult will hire us to solve a mystery? Adults don't ask kids for help."

"They'll come around once they see how good we are!" Malena asserted enthusiastically. She looked over at Hector. "You ready?"

Hector lifted both hands over the keyboard and cocked his head to the side. He looked like a dog listening intently.

"Okay." Malena began to count off what they knew on her fingers, "First, we have the ghost. Casey talked about fog, cold water, and the thing that tried to grab him."

"Don't forget about the pool glowing green," Natsumi added.

Kimmey tilted her head and sighed out of frustration. "How is that even possible?"

Malena kept her eyes on the table, thinking. The rest of the League grew quiet while waiting for her expectantly.

"I believe Casey," she said finally, raising her eyes to look at each member separately. "I think he honestly believes he saw a glowing green ghost, but that doesn't mean that's what happened. Why not narrow down the possibilities before saying, 'I give up. It's impossible!' That's just lazy."

Kimmey grimaced at the truth of Malena's words. She nodded in reluctant agreement.

"What do you think he saw?" John asked.

"We don't know, but let's come up with some possibilities of what it *could* have been. After that, we'll see if any of those are more likely than an actual glowing green ghost."

Everything was quiet for a moment except for the clicking sound of Hector's keyboard. His eyes were intent upon the computer screen, his ears sensitive to Malena's confident words. He was not disappointed with their systematic plan of action.

"If we solve the mystery," Malena began, her eyes shining at the possibility, "this will be big. Right now, the school's top swimmer is on dry land. There's a big swim meet coming up, and that means tempers are going to flare. It's really, really important that Casey be able to swim again. It's not just about him—it's about the entire school, kids and parents and teachers are involved. If we can solve this, we'll prove that we are the real thing."

Unimpressed, Kimmey asked dryly, "And how do you propose we carry out this plan?"

"We should split up. Each person will use their core field of science to examine the mystery. Kimmey and Natsumi, you try to find a way to duplicate Casey's ghost. See if you can make the fog, the cold, the green glowing water and the orange tentacles." She turned to Hector and waited until he finished typing to continue. "Hector, I want you to talk to Casey. Find out what actually happened, not just what's currently circulating on the rumor mill."

"What can I do to help?" John asked.

Malena turned her big brown eyes on him and smiled.

"Can you swim?"

CHAPTER 8

John and Malena wasted no time in fulfilling their part of the investigation. That Saturday, they met at the pool during community swim. Half the pool was open to the public, the other half was team practice since the competition was getting closer.

After changing into their swimsuits, they found themselves standing at the edge of the deep end. John thought of Casey's description of a vacant, glowing pool. For some reason, he had expected it to still be empty of swimmers and green. But it wasn't.

The pool was alive. It was packed with kids who were diving, swimming and hanging out in the water with their friends in the water. Loud echoes of the yelling and splashing were periodically interrupted by Coach Warren's whistle.

"You were worried," Malena teased. "This isn't so bad, right? If the ghost is going to get us, it's got to eat a lot of other kids first."

"Yeah," John said sarcastically. "I feel better now."

He realized Malena hadn't heard. She was already walking toward the swim lanes on the far side of the pool.

"Good thing Coach Warren is here," Malena said. "We can ask him some questions."

"Why?" John followed Malena.

"Because Casey said that Coach Warren was late for that morning's practice, and he's never late. So, where was he on the one morning the ghost decided to scare Casey?"

John looked sharply at Malena. "You think Coach Warren is the ghost?"

"Maybe. Though, I don't know why he'd want to scare his star swimmer away from the water. He's a nice guy and a good coach."

"Why would he want to hurt the swim team?" John asked.

Malena was quiet a moment, thinking. "I don't think he would. I don't think he's the ghost. But he might be able to tell us something new."

They rounded the corner of the pool, and Malena stopped in front of the dull silver pool ladder. She set her towel down a few feet away from the edge so as not to soak it in the leftover puddles from the swimmers who just got out. John followed suit.

"First things first," Malena said. "Let's check out where it happened."

She stepped onto the top rung of the ladder, turned, and quickly dropped herself into the pool. Beneath the water, her floating black hair waved like kelp. She popped her head up and blew out a breath. Then she moved away from the ladder and looked up at John impatiently.

"Well? Come on!"

"Is it cold?"

"Bathwater."

John dipped his toes in.

"Baths are a ton warmer than this. *Ice* is a lot warmer than this . . ."

Treading water with just her legs, Malena splashed him.

John gasped, feeling the water douse his legs like an ice-cold hand. He stood there shivering as Malena laughed.

"Sorry John. Couldn't help it."

"I wouldn't have done that to you!"

Malena stopped laughing and looked at John soberly. "No, you wouldn't have, would you?" she said thoughtfully.

John turned away from Malena's uncomfortable gaze, grabbed the ladder rails, and slowly lowered himself into the water. He sucked in air through his teeth as he tried to get used to the cold.

Malena swam closer.

"Sorry John. I was just playing."

"It's okay."

"Come on. Let's check out where Casey said all this happened."

Malena swam down the lane in a slow side stroke, and John followed her in a doggy paddle. A few strokes later, she stopped. John's arms were tired already. Once they were at the end of the lane, he lurched toward the side of the pool to grab the edge so he could rest.

Something pushed at his stomach. Thinking about the orange tentacles, John yelped.

"What is it?" Malena asked as she swam toward him.

"Something ..." John murmured in confusion, as he frantically looked down.

"It's just the pool filter." Malena grabbed John's hand under the water and held it over the small nozzle mounted on the pool wall. He felt a driving force of rushing water push his fingers away from the nozzle. When he moved his hand away, he could see a visible jet of water streaming through the pool's relatively stagnant water. John put his hand in front of the stream, this time several inches away from the nozzle. The water still pummeled against it but not as hard as before because of the distance.

Malena watched John carefully. As he played with the stream of water, she said, "All big pools have these, you know. They've got to suck out the dirty water and put clean water back in. You don't spend a lot of time in pools, do you?"

"It's been a while since I went swimming. Like, years."

Malena's eyes grew wide. "You're kidding?"

"I'm just not a big swimmer. My mom used to take me to Meyers Lake. But we don't live there anymore. I can't even remember the last time I was in a pool."

Malena nodded, accepting his story. She averted her attention when something caught her eye. Malena stuck out both arms and did a fancy kick with her legs, making her spin in a circle. "This is where Casey said the ghost was."

"Here?" John asked a little too loud. He swallowed nervously as he peered down into the water. "Do you think he really did see a ghost?"

"I'm sure he thinks he saw a ghost, but it was probably just his imagination," Malena said. "I mean, it seems a little far-fetched to me. Don't you agree?"

"Maybe," John said wearily as he kept his eyes trained on the water.

Malena laughed. "There's nothing here, John."

He felt himself blush. “I know,” he said quickly. John looked at his arms slung over the side of the pool. They were still wet. Goose bumps dotted his skin as he shivered. “I’m cold.”

“Well, you’re not exactly moving. Bodies generate more heat while in motion. That’s why I’m warmer than you right now.”

“Malena!” John exclaimed. “Casey was doing laps when he saw the ghost, wasn’t he?”

“I think so. I heard he’d been practicing for awhile,” Malena said.

“So that means his body would have been generating a lot of heat, right? If he felt cold, it must have been because he really *did* feel cold water.”

A slow grin spread across Malena’s face. She swam toward John and grabbed the edge of the pool. “I think you’re right, John.”

John smiled smugly. “So, now that I’ve proved myself to be a genius….”

Malena laughed. “Oh, I wouldn’t say that just yet. Come on. Let’s go talk to Coach Warren. There isn’t anything peculiar about the pool as far as I can tell.”

They climbed out of the pool, water splattering from their bodies and onto the tiled floor.

Wrapping their towels around them, John and Malena walked to the other end of the huge pool. There, the East Rapids swimmers were practicing their diving. The coach stood off to the side of the diving board, watching as a line of swimmers took turns on the board and rocketed themselves into the water.

Coach Warren was a big, muscular man. Even from a distance, John could see his tan arms bulging beneath a baby blue t-shirt. His bald head reflected the fluorescent lights making it look shiny. He had faint stubble on his chin, which made him look even more intimidating. John began to second-guess their decision to speak with him. Malena, on the other hand, had been under Coach Warren's supervision when she played on the girls' Junior Varsity soccer team last spring. With nothing to fear, she marched boldly up to him.

"Excuse me," Malena called out. "Coach Warren?"

"Yes?" The coach glanced at them briefly before turning back to the pool.

"Did Casey really see a ghost?" Malena asked excitedly. John's head jerked to look at her in disbelief. John shook his head in awe. *She really likes to get straight to the point.*

The coach laughed and crossed his arms. Without glancing at them, he said, "Casey's blown the whole thing out of proportion. There's no ghost."

"But what did he see if it wasn't a ghost?" Malena asked.

Coach Warren sighed, rubbing a hand along his shiny forehead. "I don't know," he said in quiet resignation. Then his voice grew louder and firmer, "What I do know is that his paranoia is hurting the rest of the team. Casey refuses to enter the water, and the other kids aren't swimming as well as they used to because they're too worried about seeing a ghost. That, or they're busy teasing each other. It's not good for morale, at any rate."

"Do you think someone was playing a prank on Casey? He's pretty popular, isn't he?" Malena asked innocently.

"He's my best swimmer," Coach Warren said simply. "His teammates would have known better than to pull a prank like this."

Malena glanced over at John and then back at Coach Warren. "But why weren't you at the pool that morning? You're always one of the first people at the school each day."

Coach Warren apparently didn't like this line of questioning. He adopted a steely stare. "I had a flat," he stated simply, adding no details.

Alerted by his defensive tone, Malena collected herself to continue her questioning.

"What happened?"

Coach Warren's tense stance, however, did not relax. John looked anxiously between Malena and the intimidating coach. He wished he had telepathy.

He knows we're questioning his motive and alibi, Malena.

"My car tire lost air overnight. Now, get out of here," Coach Warren said, suddenly annoyed. "I'm trying to coach, and I'm about to think you two were the ones that let the air out of my tire."

"Someone let the air out of your tire?" Malena exclaimed. She made eye contact with John for a moment. "Why would someone do that?"

"I don't know," Coach Warren said bitingly. "Now why don't you go harass someone else, huh?"

Noticing Malena wasn't about to back down, John decided to back down for her. "Sorry," he said quickly to Coach Warren, seizing Malena's arm. John dragged her towards the exit in order to get away from the very tall, very muscular, and very agitated coach. As soon as they were out of earshot, John whispered, "Someone let the air out of his tire so he wouldn't see the ghost!"

"But who would do that?" Malena asked.

"I guess that's what we have to find out, huh?" John tilted his head and looked at Malena. She laughed and wrapped an arm around John's shoulders, leading him towards the exit.

"I'm glad you decided to join the League," she said.

John felt like he was glowing. Trying to reign in a huge smile, he replied, "And I'm glad you asked me!"

They stopped outside the locker rooms. Removing her arm from around John's shoulder, Malena looked him up and down once. "I have a new mystery for you to solve, John."

"Piece of cake."

Malena laughed. "Awfully confident now, aren't we? Anyway, here's the thing I'm trying to figure out."

"Shoot."

"You said you haven't been swimming in years, right?"

"I haven't."

"Then why does your swimsuit fit you perfectly? It doesn't look like an old swimsuit to me."

"It's new. I just got it," John said.

"You bought a new swimsuit? Just for today? You didn't have to spend—"

"But I wanted to come. And, well, you asked me."

Malena smiled. "You shouldn't be spending money, though. Who knows when we'll need it?"

John laughed and turned to go into the locker room. "I'll meet you outside," he called over his shoulder.

"Then we can go back to the Lab and see if Hector has finished interviewing Casey yet."

After changing back into their clothes, John and Malena left the gym talking. They were so focused on their conversation that they didn't stop to look around. If they had, they would've seen something important. Something that was out of place. At the far side of the pool near the maintenance closet, hidden by rickety metal stairs, a shadow moved. It listened. And with two bright, sinister eyes, it watched.

CHAPTER 9

Hector rang the doorbell. Somewhere from deep inside the bowels of the house, he heard chimes playing classical music. He'd heard the tune before, but he couldn't name it.

"Yes?" A woman's voice spoke from an intercom above the doorbell.

"Oh, uh…hi, Mrs. Keller? I'm Hector Alejandro Manuel. I'm here to see Casey."

"I'll tell him you're here."

After a few moments, the door swung open. Casey stood just inside with a look of surprise on his face.

"Hey, Hector. What's up, dude?"

"Not a whole lot."

They stood there in silence for an awkward moment. Hector cleared his throat and hoisted his bag over his shoulder. "I really just want to know more about the ghost," Hector confessed.

Casey stepped back and slowly dropped his smile into a frown.

"Wow. That was pretty blunt."

Hector grimaced. He wasn't very good at conversation, so Hector thought he should just tell Casey the real reason for his visit. "Sorry," he finally said. "It's okay if you don't want to talk."

Casey thought about it. "No," he said. "It's cool. I just don't want to be surprised anymore. You know?"

"Yeah, I know," Hector reassured Casey. Actually, Hector didn't have any idea what Casey meant, but Casey seemed willing to talk, so Hector went with it. Casey motioned Hector inside the mansion and began to talk as he closed the door behind them.

"Everyone thinks I'm nuts or that I just want attention. Even my best buddy, Kyle ," Casey paused seeing Hector's confused look. "Kyle VanderJack. He doesn't go to our school. He laughed at me! Some friend," Casey ended glumly.

"Where's he going to school?" Hector asked. They were walking deeper into the home. Their steps on the marble floor sent echoes through the imperial-style hall. Hector felt out of place and grungy while set against the polished banisters and expensive décor. He just remembered that he'd been wearing his black hoodie for the last three days. He casually ducked his head to fit his nose under the collar to make sure it didn't smell.

"He goes to West Shore. He's on their swim team. We compete in the municipal league together in the summer. That's how we met," Casey said, leading him to the end of a hallway.

Hector quickly glanced at what Casey was wearing. He noticed with relief that Casey's jeans had holes in them. Hector felt infinitely better.

"You wanna go downstairs?" Casey offered as he opened a door. "We can talk more in the den."

Hector followed Casey down a set of stairs. The staircase was twice as long as a normal one. The walls were cream-colored, accented by family photographs and pictures of Casey swimming or holding up medals. Hector thought the photographs were a nice touch, especially with the display lighting. They transformed an architectural museum into a home.

As they reached the bottom of the stairs, Hector saw a pitch black, empty door frame that opened up into what he supposed was the den. Hector felt a new sensation slipping over him. The mood was darker. Casey flicked a wall switch and led Hector into the room. As they entered the den, a single overhead light struggled into action. The flickering created an erratic white and ghostly, and then dark and eerie, light show. Hector could hardly believe this was part of the same house.

Deep red curtains boxed in the room and kept any sunlight from seeping in. The flickering light bulb made the curtained walls appear to ooze gelatinously down to the floor as if it were a wall of blood. Hector felt goose bumps prick his skin.

"Welcome to my room," Casey said magnanimously. He sat down on a black futon across from a big-screen TV. The TV glowed a sickly blue.

"Your parents let you decorate your room like this?" Hector could hardly believe this gloomy room existed in a house fit for royalty. It was more like a dungeon than a den.

"It's *my* room," Casey said, his wide eyes set intensely on Hector daring him to comment on his choice of décor.

Unnerved, Hector made a point of sitting at the other end of the futon. "My parents never come down here anyway. It creeps them out." Casey made air quotations when he said "creeps".

Hector laughed. "I wonder why," he said sarcastically. His gaze fell on Casey's collection of DVDs. Many of the titles had ominous red lettering or pictures of zombies on the covers. Most of the DVDs were arranged neatly on the shelves of the TV stand, but others had spilled over as though they'd been regurgitated.

Hector glanced over at Casey. The dead blue of the TV screen cast shadows on his face making his eyes look sunken and his overall complexion dreadfully ill. "That's quite a movie collection you have," Hector pointed towards them.

"Thanks," Casey replied. "I have more digitally if you wanna see."

"That's okay," Hector said quickly. He glanced back over at the movie titles: *Massacre of the Undead, Eyes Without A Face, The Evil Dead, etc...* "I think I'll pass." Hector turned his head to look at his host before asking, "Don't you watch anything normal?"

"Pretty much the only things I watch are horror films," he said.

"How do you sleep at night?" Hector asked in wonder. He glanced at the corner of the room where Casey's bed sat in shadow, far from the flickering light. It almost looked like there was a body there, hunched beneath the blankets, waiting, just waiting ...

Casey laughed abruptly. "I don't know, man. I'm tough!"

"What about that ghost you saw?" Hector asked.

"That was real!" Casey exclaimed, suddenly passionate. "Everyone thinks I'm overreacting or that I just imagined it. I know what I saw. I was *not* imagining it."

"But what did you really see? There are a few different versions of your story floating around now."

Casey's eyes were wide, the whites intensely visible around his dark irises. The rest of his face was bathed in shadow. Hector shivered. Casey began to gesture with his hands as he spoke, "There was a fog. It was rolling off the water like … like … Have you seen *Gone Away Lake*?"

Hector shook his head.

"It was sort of like what happens in that movie. There's this really heavy fog that settles over the lake one night. It starts to twist into weird shapes—kind of like what happened to me, right? And the shapes visit the townspeople at midnight, and . . . and . . . it's just really, really intense. That's why it was so freaky when it happened to me. It was like *déjà vu* or something!"

"You saw shapes in the fog?"

"Kind of," Casey said. "I mean, it went beneath the water, like it became a hand—or claw—or something. Anyway, it was trying to grab me, and the air was so cold, but the water was steaming! I swear, the water looked like it was boiling, but it was *freezing,*" Casey shivered visibly. "I've never been so scared in my life," he confessed. Casey paused in his tale and gave Hector a sideways glance. "I'm a pretty brave guy. You can see that. I mean, just look at the movies I watch!"

"But…a ghost? Why jump to that conclusion so quickly?"

"What else could it be?" Casey asked curtly. "When I tried to swim away, it—it reached for me. It didn't grab me or anything, but whatever it was, it was close. I remember looking at it as the sun shone right into the pool." Fear slowly filled his eyes as he remembered, and he appeared drained. "I remember seeing it *glow.* That freaked me out the worst—the glow."

Hector looked around the basement furtively, keeping his eyes away from the darker corners. The overhead light still did its best to keep the dark at bay. It hummed and flickered, making shadows dance around the room to a lifeless tune. Casey watched Hector seriously with such a nauseated expression that Hector almost felt sick.

Finally, Hector said, "You really did see a ghost, didn't you?"

"I don't know what else it could have been," Casey replied. "That's the only thing that makes sense."

***

Hector sat with the rest of the League back at the Lab. He filled everyone in on his interview with Casey.

"The next time someone has to go to Casey's house, I'd prefer it be anyone but me," Hector shivered at the memory.

Kimmey laughed teasingly. "Why not? You don't like being a private investigator?"

"Actually, I like that part a lot. But I don't like being scared, and Casey's den is certifiably, one-hundred-percent scary. I have no idea how he watches those movies down there. It's creepy."

"So," Malena began, "when you guys talked about the ghost—"

"He's so dead-set on whatever he saw." Hector's eyes widened with passion. "You should have seen him when he told me about it. Just remembering it freaked him out."

"Do you think he really saw a ghost?" John asked.

Hector bit his lip, thinking. After a moment, he said, "I don't know, honestly. I don't know what else it could be. Whatever it is, though, I kind of think Casey *wants* it to be a ghost. With all the freaky movies he watches, I think ghosts just naturally pop into his brain. If all you do is watch horror movies and then you see something weird in real life, of course you're going to think it's something supernatural."

"He'll never find the truth that way. Never assume," Natsumi sagely said. "It's easier to guess, but you could be wrong."

Natsumi met Kimmey's eyes as though they were having a telepathic conversation. Kimmey turned to look at the others to share what she and Natsumi had come up with. "We've got ideas as to what this 'ghost' might be. But we need to do some more research before we can say anything for sure."

"Me, too," Hector agreed. "There's someone else I want to talk to."

"Who?" Malena asked.

"Kyle VanderJack. Casey's friend. He swims for the West Shore team. I wonder if he's involved with this somehow."

"Can't hurt to ask him, right?" Malena shrugged.

"Yeah," Hector said. "As long as he doesn't invite me into his basement!"

CHAPTER 10

Kimmey and Natsumi had become so immersed with all the ghost theories that they hardly talked about anything else. Natsumi didn't even get excited when her parents took her for her favorite meal at *Use Your Noodle!*

Their heads were filled with chemicals and solutions, anything they thought could possibly have something to do with changing water temperature and color. Kimmey's parents thought it was odd at first that she and Natsumi were constantly working on science experiments. After hearing about Casey's swimming pool drama, Kimmey's parents realized that this was the likely motivation for the girls' extracurricular science activities. Of course, they didn't want to discourage the girls' ambition, particularly when it was supplementing their education so well. But there were only so many chemical abbreviations Mr. and Mrs. Pryce could take during dinner.

Trying to escape the periodic table that was spilling out of the girls' mouths, Mr. and Mrs. Pryce suggested they go see the new sci-fi movie that had just been released.

"It's called *Elda and the TekMage,*" Mr. Pryce shared.

"I hear it got good reviews," Mrs. Pryce added.

It was only after Kimmey's parents assured them that seeing this movie would give them a new perspective on the case, she and Natsumi agreed to go.

Sitting towards the back with a large popcorn and two medium drinks, they were bombarded by images of dark forests, a running woman, and brilliant flashes of green lightning.

Kimmey elbowed Natsumi and whispered, "Hey. Give me some popcorn."

Natsumi handed over the popcorn bucket, her wide eyes never moving from the screen.

Kimmey took one glance inside the popcorn bucket and groaned, "You ate it all!"

"There's still a little there," Natsumi said absently, still staring unblinkingly at the movie screen.

"Yeah, kernels," Kimmey retorted accusingly.

"Shhh!" Natsumi leaned forward in her chair in concentration.

Kimmey sighed and began to search around the bottom of the bucket. She uncovered a few half-popped pieces, which she promptly threw into her mouth. Natsumi sensed Kimmey's lack of interest.

"You're missing the good stuff," Natsumi whispered.

Kimmey gave an exaggerated yawn. "I'm bored. We should've gotten candy. I like those sour chewy things. Hector said they all taste the same but I like the red ones—"

"Shhh!" Natsumi cut her off, lifting a hand to stop her from talking.

"What is it?" Kimmey asked. Natsumi *never* interrupted anyone, not unless it was important.

Natsumi pointed at the screen. "See anything interesting?"

Kimmey watched.

The movie's final scene was a high-tech, special-effects-filled fight. Elda, with her nature magic, pulled down lightning bolts to attack Brand, the TekMage. She followed her attack with the TekMage's worst enemy—water—in the form of a torrential rainstorm. The water flew through the air so fast it moved sideways. It struck the TekMage, damaging his power suit and causing it to spark and crack. Some of the cracks leaked, glowing green ooze.

Kimmey looked at Natsumi expectantly, thinking she had an idea from the glowing green ooze, but then realized Natsumi wasn't watching the fight. Instead, her eyes were focused on the bottom of the movie screen.

Kimmey followed Natsumi's gaze and saw the fog. It swirled around the screen, keeping low, always moving, twisting and changing as the actors jumped through it. After staring intensely at the fog, Kimmey imagined she could see strange shapes in it. She turned to Natsumi in excitement over their breakthrough.

"We need to find out more about these special effects," Kimmey whispered. "They might teach us how to make a ghost."

Natsumi nodded, her brow furrowing as she continued to watch the fog.

***

Kimmey and Natsumi ran from the theater the moment the credits began. Out in the parking lot, they found Mr. Pryce's car and headed towards it. As they climbed in, Mr. Pryce said, "Hey girls, how was the movie?"

Kimmey and Natsumi were lost in thought and didn't answer. Mr. Pryce turned around in the seat to look at them.

"Hey!" Mr. Pryce waved his hand in front of their faces. "Hello? Everything okay?"

"Yeah, Dad," Kimmey said. "Sorry, we were just trying to figure something out."

Natsumi spoke up, "There were some special effects in the movie that might help us on the case."

"Really? Like what?"

Mr. Pryce was one of the few adults who knew about the League of Scientists ever since Kimmey had asked permission to turn their shed into the League's lab. Mrs. Pryce just thought the League worked on puzzles and science experiments, but Mr. Pryce knew the truth. In fact, after Kimmey had told him about it, he looked like he'd wanted to join. He loved watching old detective shows on TV and was always eager to help Kimmey and her friends with any mystery.

"Well," Kimmey said. "There was this scene with a bunch of fog. How do you make fog?"

Mr. Pryce laughed. "Well, you could do it the old-fashioned way—just make things really humid. That's how nature does it."

"No, Dad, this was different. It was really thick. You could walk through it, and it would swirl around and stuff."

Mr. Pryce thought for a moment. "There are a few different ways. If you mix up the right chemicals, you could make a fog. They use chemical smoke machines in concerts and movies. We even used them when I acted back in college. They were great for making a scary, heavy fog. It would sink to the ground, stay for a while, and they looked pretty cool. That's probably what you saw today unless it was computer-generated."

“Sweet! Let’s get a smoke machine!” Kimmey exclaimed. Kimmey quickly turned to Natsumi to share her reasoning, “If someone did make Casey’s ghost, maybe they used one of those.”

“Uh, no,” Mr. Pryce answered immediately, talking over Kimmey and Natsumi’s budding conversation. “I’m not about to buy a smoke machine. Those are expensive. Plus, they stink.”

“Oh,” Kimmey said, dejectedly.

“There are other ways,” Mr. Pryce continued. “Like dry ice. That’s cheap and easy to find. I’ll get some for you if you promise to use it carefully. There’s fire, too. When certain things burn, they kick up more smoke than others. That could be your fog.”

“I think,” Kimmey deliberated, “we need to do more research. I want to find something that looked like what we saw in the movie.”

“Here,” Mr. Pryce said, reaching over to hand her his tablet. “Search away.”

Kimmey hunched over the tablet and began typing quickly on the keyboard.

“Also, look up glowing slime,” Natsumi said. “The stuff that came out of Brand’s power suit, did you notice how it was green? And glowing?”

“Yeah,” Kimmey affirmed, still staring down at the tablet. “But that looked fake to me. Like CGI.”

“Computer effects?” Natsumi asked.

“Try looking up how to make stuff glow,” Natsumi said, leaning over Kimmey’s shoulder to look at the tablet screen.

“How to make stuff fluoresce,” Mr. Pryce said.

Kimmey looked up. “What?”

“The word you’re looking for is ‘fluoresce’. When something fluoresces, that means it glows as a response to excitement from another energy source. For example, on stage, we'd use fluorescent paint with special ultraviolet lighting. The paint would absorb the UV light and re-emit it at a visible wavelength, making it glow. You'd get this cool ghostly look where a prop could glow without the audience seeing any other lights."

Natsumi considered this, then added, "Let's try searching 'fluorescent paint' or 'fluorescent liquid.'"

"Okay." Kimmey continued typing and paging through results.

Natsumi watched over Kimmey's shoulder and spoke. "This could help a lot. We just need to find all the possibilities, all the different ways of making what we want. Then we rule out what we can. Like, Casey saw the ghost in the pool, so we know we need something that's safe in water."

"Okay, okay," Mr. Pryce interrupted the girls before they could pick up their chemical conversation from dinner. "Enough about smoke and slime! What did you girls think of the *movie*?"

"Do you even know the storyline?" Kimmey asked, her eyes still focused on the tablet screen in front of her.

"I've heard a little about it."

"Oh. Well, it was okay, I guess," Kimmey said. Natsumi nodded in agreement.

"Just *okay*?" he asked, looking at them askance in the rear view mirror. "Are you kidding me? What about that ending? Will Brand ever trust Elda after what she did? And what if Elda delivers the First Computer back to the Worldnet?"

Kimmey stopped typing and slowly lifted her head. She and Natsumi stared at Mr. Pryce.

"So," Kimmey said slowly, "you were *there*?"

He grinned. "The dads usually sit way in the back."

CHAPTER 11

After school, Hector biked furiously from East Rapids to West Shore. Clad in a light jacket, the December weather was still nice enough to bike in. But biking all the way from East to West was hard work, even on a bike. The trip took almost an hour.

He knew Kyle was on the West Shore swim team. He also checked online to make sure the team practiced that day. If all went according to plan, the team would still be there when Hector arrived.

He pedaled up to West Shore and skidded sideways to a rubber-shredding halt. Then he locked his bike and went into the gym.

The smell of sweat and chlorine punched Hector in the nose. He closed his eyes, inhaled, and turned slowly in a circle, trying to detect where the chlorine smell was coming from. He wondered if, like a bloodhound, he would be able to sniff out the pool. He had decided to sample the air near a pair of blue doors when a man's deep voice interrupted.

"Can I help you?"

Hector turned to face the speaker, not because of the words themselves, but because of the way the voice sounded. It had the slightly annoyed, overly-polite attitude he'd heard from other adults in a position of authority. It made Hector feel that someone was trying to get rid of him as soon as possible.

Hector sized the man up. He was slender and had mocha-colored skin. His black shoes shone and his red tie stood out against his black shirt and jacket. His salt and pepper hair was slicked back, and he reeked of cologne. The guy probably worked at the school, and he clearly had an important job. He dressed too nicely to be a teacher.

The man looked at Hector, staring, his mouth pulled into a tight-lipped smile. One hand tapped impatiently against his leg, giving away his attempted politeness.

Hector knew how to handle this. He knew what people saw when they looked at him: a short kid in dark clothes and a baseball cap. They made assumptions, and from these assumptions, Hector drew a sort of power. If this guy wanted to treat him like a punk immigrant kid, then that's what he'd be. To convince the man otherwise might take too long. He probably wouldn't believe Hector anyway.

Hector adopted a dull, glazed expression. He let his eyes grow soft, and hung his mouth open.

"*Si,*" he drawled. "I'm supposed to be at the pool?"

"You're not on the swim team," the man accused, looking

Hector up and down. His eyes narrowed. "You're not even a student here, are you?"

"*No, Señor,*" Hector said. "Just visiting. I'm supposed to meet Kyle VanderJack after swim practice."

Hector looked up at the man hopefully, figuring that if he knew the name of an actual West Shore student, the man would help—if only to get Hector out of his way.

The man shot his wrist out of a suit cuff and looked at his watch. It was nice, Hector noticed. It was one of those big, expensive-looking ones, with a lot of shiny moving parts. Hector preferred small, compact watches with built-in tools: barometers, altimeters, thermostats, pulse monitors and computer ports. A watch that could only tell time was a sad waste of a wrist. The man might as well have strapped a sundial to his arm.

The man slid his gleaming watch back under his cuff and sighed.

"Fine," he said. "Follow me."

The man had long legs, and he wasn't shy about using them. Hector had to hurry to keep up.

A short hallway maze later, the man held open a large metal door for Hector and then followed him through. Hector stepped into the West Shore pool area. The swim team was still there, practicing.

"Here we are," the man stopped behind Hector. Something in his voice made Hector turn back and look at him.

"Now," the man said, smiling sardonically, "can you tell me which swimmer is Kyle VanderJack?"

Hector looked at the man, surprised, then back at the mass of swimmers in the pool. He had no clue what Kyle looked like. Staying in character, Hector turned away from the man and began walking toward the pool.

“Hey,” the man said, jogging to catch Hector, his expensive shoes knocking on the tile floor, “You can’t go—”

“Kyle!”

Hector yelled loud enough so everyone in the pool could hear.

Give them all a stimulus. Watch for the right response. His eyes flicked around the pool, watching the swimmers. They all stopped and were staring at him. Hector knew a number of things could go wrong with this plan, particularly if there were more than one Kyle on the swim team.

“What?” one student yelled from the water. Hector felt an instant relaxation in his tense stance. *It worked.* He studied the kid who answered him. Kyle had thick brown eyebrows that hung heavy below his blue swim cap, but otherwise he had a friendly face.

When Hector took a step towards the swimmers to talk to Kyle, the man grabbed his arm. “Hey, I don’t want you interrupting our practice,” he said. “You can wait quietly against the wall for your friend to finish.” The man then turned on his heels and headed for what looked like an office. The man looked as if he was dancing awkwardly, as his shoes slipped on the wet pool tiles.

Hector dropped his face back into the sullen look he had worn before. This time he wasn’t acting. Hector really didn’t like this guy who looked like he’d rather be anywhere but at the pool. Hector shook his head disapprovingly, wondering why the man, who Hector now assumed was the swim coach, dressed so slick at a pool. It seemed silly to get all dressed up when you’d be splashed and had no choice but to step in puddles of chlorine water to get anywhere. Hector just dressed to be comfortable. To Hector, clothes were just clothes.

“Kyle,” Hector called to the boy staring up at him from the water. “We need to talk about Casey.”

Kyle's eyebrows lowered a little in confusion. He stared up at Hector quizzically. Finally, he slowly replied, "Yeah, sure. Just let me finish this run."

Another student swam over. She was a red-haired girl with slivers of her bangs that managed to wiggle out from under her cap. She looked ready to burst into laughter. "You said Casey? Casey Keller?! The East Rapids kid who's scared of the water?" Then she laughed like a hyena. "What are *you* here for? To try and scare *us* away like Casey?" Hector knew the girl was taunting him by her guffaws that echoed off the pool walls. He tried to keep the peace anyways.

"No, I just want to talk to Kyle—"

"Where's the ghost, kid? Come on!" She motioned for her teammates to join in on her revelry. "*Where's the ghost*?" She began a chant.

One by one, other students joined in, calling out in unison with the redheaded girl. Apparently, Casey's story had already reached the entire West Shore swim team. Other students in the far end of the pool stopped their swimming and began to yell between bouts of laughter.

"Where's the ghost? Where's the ghost?"

Their chanting grew louder.

"Where's The Ghost? Where's The Ghost?"

One big voice echoed around the pool, the sound bouncing off the walls. Hector winced at the noise.

"WHERE'S THE GHOST???"

The few students who ignored the revelry had been practicing diving drills in the deep end. Hearing all the commotion, the coach stormed back into the room. As he approached, one of the students stepped onto the high dive, and, probably distracted by all that was going on, slipped. His feet flew out from under him and then his head crashed—hard—onto the diving board. His body fell into the water and did not resurface.

Hector saw it happen out of the corner of his eye.

"Someone help!"

Hector didn't know who had screamed, but it was like throwing a bucket of cold water on the group's merrymaking. The atmosphere turned from mockery to icy fear in an instant. The swimmers in the pool all began to swim frantically toward the student now floating face down in the water. Hector couldn't move, paralyzed by what he'd just witnessed.

It took a moment for the coach to realize one of his students was floating lifelessly in the pool. In the movies, when someone's stuck in the water, the hero always takes off his shoes and strips off his jacket before diving in to save the day. This man didn't do any of that. Fully clothed, he moved to the edge of the pool and dove straight in.

The coach torpedoed under the water, angling toward the student like a hungry shark. He surfaced nearby and pulled the student's head out of the water. He crooked an arm around the boy's torso and swam with the unconscious boy toward the pool's edge. Other students hurried across the tiles to meet them. Reaching out their arms, they helped pull their teammate and then their coach to safety.

As the boy was pulled from the water, he began to wake up. He moaned and coughed up water while the coach hunched over him and gently pushed hair out of the boy's face.

"You'll be fine, Ethan. Knocked you silly there for a minute, didn't it? Let's get you cleaned up and we'll see a doctor."

Dripping wet, the man helped Ethan sit up. Water from his fancy clothes splattered the ground and dribbled down his expensive watch and onto his shiny shoes as he stood up with Ethan. Everything he wore was ruined.

Hector knew he'd made a mistake about judging the well-tailored coach. The coach's appearance had tricked Hector just as easily as Hector's "immigrant kid" act had tricked the coach. When the time came, out of the two of them, the real man was the one who dove into the pool. The coach of West Shore, fancy clothes and all, had earned Hector's full respect.

***

"Okay, *that* was freaky."

Kyle VanderJack stood next to Hector and peeled the swim cap from his head. Shaggy brown hair spilled out and into his eyes. Kyle grinned at Hector.

"Yeah," Hector said, still a little shell shocked. "I hope he's okay."

"Me, too. He's one of our better swimmers."

The girl who had started the ghost chant was standing next to Kyle. She gave him a death glare. Kyle took a step back and raised his hands.

"What?"

"That's messed up, Kyle," she said reproachfully. "You thought it was so funny when you told us about Casey and his 'ghost.' Now Ethan's hurt—really hurt—and you don't care enough to make sure he's okay?"

"He's fine," Kyle replied, unmoved. He pointed to where the coach was helping the injured swimmer across the pool towards the exit. "Coach Gavin's taking care of him."

"Not that you care," the girl accused. "You care more about the team than the people on it."

Kyle rolled his eyes at his teammate and motioned for Hector to walk with him . . . away from the redhead. It was the end of practice, and Kyle needed to finish his chemistry project. Kyle got Hector's number and promised to call later before he headed out.

Disappointed that he didn't get a chance to speak with Kyle and still rattled from the traumatic incident, Hector left West

Shore. He slowly pedaled home. Usually, he wore earphones to listen to music while he biked, but today he didn't. Instead he used the ride home to think. What the girl had said to Kyle kept echoing in his mind.

"You care more about the team than the people on it."

CHAPTER 12

John saw it coming. Dowser had been paying too much attention to him all day. Even as they walked out of the school doors, John felt Dowser staring daggers at his back. When he looked over his shoulder, Dowser made sure John saw him speed up. John quickly turned around and began to run. When Dowser started chasing him, he was terrified, and his sole focus was getting away. Panting hard, blasting past house after house, his body shifted into a panicked autopilot as he ran for all that he was worth.

He didn't know what to do. He'd never been chased before, at least not like this. It was like a horrible problem from Mr.

Elinger's Algebra class: *If a bully runs at 15 miles per hour and is 200 feet behind a student running 12 miles per hour, how soon will John get beaten to a pulp?*

He knew the answer: *Soon.*

He should never have left the school, not with Dowser blatantly following him. At least at school, he would've been safe. *Safe,* he thought. *Somewhere safe...*

John sped past pockets of forests and neighbors' bushes that all looked like a streak of jungle. His mind flashed to the nature shows he'd seen. He thought of a cheetah leaping on top of a gazelle. Just once, he'd like to see the gazelle fight back and win. But if not, maybe he could do something different, something unexpected. In the predator-prey relationship, the gazelles always ran. As John ran, he realized he didn't have to. He was human—of higher intelligence than animals. He could disappear instead.

When John skidded around the corner of a house, he looked frantically around for somewhere to hide. A shed maybe? The bushes in the back of the yard looked like a possible spot. He stumbled toward them, stopped, and then slowly turned to look behind him—at the screened-in porch.

With sudden inspiration, he ran to the screen door, praying it would be unlocked. It was. He slid through and hunched behind a couch just as Dowser tore around the corner. He now understood one reason Dowser was on the basketball team—he was fast. Within seconds, he had smashed his way through the bushes at the edge of the yard.

John closed his eyes and ducked his head. He could hear Dowser's pounding feet, his heaving breath, and then … silence. He opened an eye and peered around the couch. Nothing. Dowser was gone.

John stayed where he was, crouched down, behind the couch with the faded flower pattern. Though his body was motionless, his heart didn't seem to realize it, and he still hadn't caught his breath. He leaned over and down, dropping his forehead to rest on a carpet of spiky, fake grass. It smelled like plastic and dirt.

"Get out of my house!"

John whirled into a sitting position and stared. An old man stood in the doorway leading from the porch to the inside of the house. He was short—John guessed about 5'4"—with a hooked nose and intelligent eyes. His legs had a weird shape to them, bowed out as if he were riding an invisible horse. In one hand, he held a watering can, in the other, a flyswatter. The man kept the flyswatter raised, held aloft by one shaking arm as if he was about to smack the biggest fly ever.

"I want you out!" the old man yelled, and the flyswatter came down. John dodged to the side as it swished toward him.

"Please," John said, holding both hands up, looking back at the lawn where Dowser had just been. "Please be quiet—I'll leave—I'm leaving—see?!"

The man paused and looked where John was looking, then back. Something crossed his face, an understanding, but instead of softening his expression, it only hardened his features. The man's fist tightened around the flyswatter, his veins bulging purple through his worn skin.

"Is that boy after you?" he growled. John nodded.

The man's jaw clenched. His words came out tight, drawn. "It don't matter how big *you* are son, and trust me, you ain't that big—there's always someone bigger. You can't rely on speed to always get you outta the way, and you can't rely on muscles to fight back. If life goes straight, you go sideways. Use your brain. If he wants a fight, you squirt karate juice all over him.

Give it a little time, and he won't be messing with you anymore."

"I don't really like sports," John mumbled, his eyes cast down.

The man huffed. "I'm not *saying* sports. I'm *saying* figure out what works for you. Use your brain, not your body. Smarter, not harder."

John was quiet. His face was warm under the man's reproach, and tears burned at the corners of his eyes. He couldn't meet the man's eyes.

"It'll be a while before you figure these things out. I can tell you, though, I know what it's like to be chased," the man's voice softened slightly. "I was like you, maybe even a little smaller. I know how important it is to have a safe place. If you need to hide on my porch, you have my permission." The man pointed the flyswatter at John, and the swatting end flapped weakly. "I'm going to talk to your parents though. They need to know what's going on."

John's emotions finally reached their peak. John knew he had to do something about Dowser, but up until now he hadn't known what. The man's rebuke shamed him, and his kindness hurt him. He wasn't used to it, so he mistook it for pity. As the man spoke, John turned for the screen door, whipped it open, and ran.

"Hey!" the old man yelled after him. "You get your parents to call me before you come here again!"

John didn't look back.

CHAPTER 13

Amos Watson sighed and lowered his flyswatter. Shaking his head sadly, he gently set the swatter and the watering can on his patio table, careful not to scratch the glass surface. Taking care of his flowers would have to wait. He wanted to see what damage those kids had done to his property.

First, there was that one hiding on his porch. He looked so scared when Mr. Watson caught him, he'd felt sorry for him. Then, before Mr. Watson could blink, the kid's eyes lit up, and he ran. Mr. Watson hadn't bothered to chase the kid. He couldn't move that fast. Besides, there was a better way to chase someone, and it didn't involve running anywhere. He knew how to hunt. Finding a couple of kids would be no problem.

He looked on the porch floor and checked the green plastic carpet for rips or tears. Next, he examined his faded flower-patterned couch. Everything looked fine. He decided to check the trees outside.

He stepped carefully off the porch, wishing the cement step wasn't so far down. As he landed, he felt double stabs of pain as his knees adjusted.

Following the line of greenery in his back yard, he stopped at the far edge. A clear break in the bushes showed where the kids had shoved through.

"Careful as an elephant," Mr. Watson grumbled to himself.

Snapped branches hung sadly. Others lay on the ground. Heavy footprints ran towards the next yard.

Mr. Watson sighed again. He'd have to splice a few branches back on. He looked a few feet to the side and smiled. At least the kids hadn't run into his favorite, most delicate plant. The masterpiece that had taken him years to design, develop, and grow.

He turned towards his house. Trudging back, he glanced up at the near corner of his roof. He saw the faint red light of the motion-sensing video camera. Spreading his arms wide, he waited a moment for the camera to see him. Then he brought both arms in and pointed at his face. The camera light blinked three times. Mr. Watson nodded once, and the camera blinked again in response.

Still working. That meant he'd gotten everything on camera. Mr. Watson smiled.

CHAPTER 14

Brandon LaMange threw the tennis ball against the living room wall. It hit with a loud *thwack* and bounced back towards him. He caught it with one hand.

He threw again, even harder.

Thwack.

He snatched the ball out of the air, this time needing two hands to grab it.

His dad would kill him if he caught him doing this. The knowledge of this was almost motivating in a sense. Brandon didn't receive a lot of attention from either of his parents, and his resentment tended to reveal itself through rebellion.

Both parents were at work, his father at the factory and his mother waitressing, which meant that he could do what he wanted. He didn't have basketball practice today, and chasing John Hawkins had served as his exercise for the day. He wasn't sure what to do with himself.

Thwack.

The phone rang and distracted him on the rebound, causing him to fumble with the ball before he caught it. He stepped into the kitchen and yanked the ringing phone off the charger.

"Yeah?"

"I'd like to speak to Brandon."

Brandon squinted, trying and failing to place the voice. It sounded like an old guy.

"Yeah, Brandon, that's me."

Thwack.

"Hello. My name is Amos Watson."

"Okay."

"You know me?"

"No."

"You should. You ran through my yard an hour ago and damaged my property. We have to talk."

Brandon didn't even notice that he dropped the tennis ball. It bounced away from him and rolled under the kitchen table.

There was no way this guy could've known who he was. Today was the first time he'd ever gone to that neighborhood. He definitely didn't know anyone named Amos Watson. Somehow, the guy had tracked him down.

Hawkins. Brandon thought, John Hawkins had something to do with this. He'd seen John and Malena at the pool snooping around. They hadn't seen him swimming, if they had they might not have stuck around as long as they did.

Maybe Brandon would ask Hawkins some questions. He just had to make sure the kid was alone, not with that Malena Curtina girl. You could tell from her eyes—you did *not* mess with her. Though she was physically small, she had a quick tongue and a sharp intellect. She intimidated Brandon, though he'd never admit that in a million years.

"I didn't do anything wrong," Brandon said. "I was just heading home from school."

"You were 'just heading home,' LaMange? Interesting. Let's talk about it. And while we are at it, let's talk about John Hawkins, too."

Brandon froze. *How did he know?*

The man talked a little longer. It wasn't more than a minute, but he said a lot. Brandon listened carefully to every word.

CHAPTER 15

The League met outside the Lab. When they got there, they found a sign taped to the door:

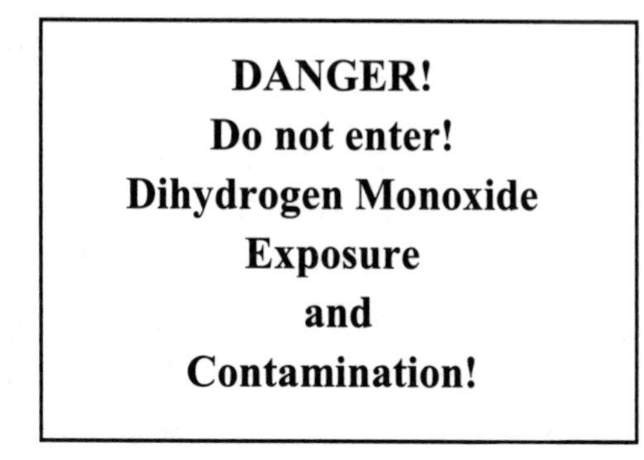

DANGER!
Do not enter!
Dihydrogen Monoxide
Exposure
and
Contamination!

Hector didn't know what Kimmey and Natsumi were up to, but he did know he didn't want to wait to find out. He paced back and forth, craning his neck as if he could somehow see around the door.

"What's in there? *¿Qué haces?"*

"Don't come in" said Kimmey. "You need to wait just like everyone else."

"You've got something cool in there, don't you?" Hector cajoled.

Kimmey's blue eyes flashed with annoyance, but Natsumi held up a hand.

"Yes," she said. "It's very cool. You will be amazed. But you see the sign? We can't have you exposed to dihydrogen monoxide!"

She smiled at Kimmey. "Not yet, anyway." Kimmey nodded, looking very serious. Hector's eyes widened, and he stepped away from the door.

Natsumi continued, "Hector, tell us about Kyle. Did he ever call you? What did you learn?"

Hector threw one last glance at the closed door. He sighed and walked back to the picnic table and sat down.

John was struck by the differences between his friends as he watched them. Hector, knowing there was information begging to be discovered behind a simple closed door, literally couldn't keep still. Kimmey's forceful method of pushing Hector away didn't change his mind, but Natsumi's gentle redirection of the subject worked perfectly. Through it all, Malena's pursed lips and smiling eyes showed she could barely contain her laughter.

They were so different, John thought, but they were all still friends. They had a lot in common and had a shared purpose in the League. He was happy here; he felt like he belonged, like he was part of a community. He felt like how he felt with his mom on Saturday trips to get ice cream or when he was concentrating hard on his robots. His new friends had become an extended family. John smiled to himself.

"No," Hector said. "Kyle never called me. He said he would, but he never did. I called his house, and he said he couldn't talk. He didn't have time. Something about a chemistry project."

"What kind of project?" Natsumi asked , passing around a plate of *anpan,* soft sweet buns filled with red bean paste. Her big brown eyes watched Hector intently. Her timidity could disguise her intelligence, but watching her now, John felt inspired by her passion.

"I didn't even get a chance to find out. I asked him, but he got off the phone too fast. Either he was telling the truth or he really didn't want to talk to me. He definitely sounded busy." Hector reached out a hand and picked at the yellow clapboard of the Lab. Looking down, he said, "I did discover something interesting, though."

"What's that?" Malena asked.

"While I was at West Shore, a kid slipped and hit his head on the diving board. That distracted me at the time, but looking back, I think I missed a bunch of clues."

He met each of his friends' eyes to ensure they were still listening. Then he continued, his voice thoughtful. "What that girl said—a girl who was talking to Kyle started a '*Where's the Ghost'* chant. I mean, the whole West Shore team knew about Casey and the ghost. It wasn't just a couple kids. There were, like, thirty students there and they all knew. The girl said that Kyle was the person who told everyone."

"That's Casey's friend, right?" Kimmey asked.

"I don't think so. Casey thinks he is, but Kyle sure doesn't act like it. The girl said Kyle was *happy* Casey saw the ghost. Kyle wasn't scared. He didn't think it was funny like he did when Casey first called to tell him about it. He was happy! I just think that's weird. It's not the right reaction. It's not what a friend would do, you know?"

"Well," John said. "He cares about the team. Maybe he's glad because it'll help them win the swim meet."

"*Claro,*" Hector said, nodding. "But I'm wondering if there's more to it than that. The way he acted, how he told West Shore about the ghost, how he won't talk to me or return my call—something's off."

"So *ask* him!" Kimmey said. "Go back to the school. Call him. Just say, 'Did you have something to do with the ghost?'"

"No," Natsumi said, shaking her head. "That's too direct. That would force Kyle into a lie."

"Why would he lie?" Hector asked, exasperated. "If we act like we know it's him, he'll admit it."

"But we don't know it's him. What if he asks for proof? There's something else, too. If Kyle is somehow responsible for the ghost, he may have been in the pool, messing with the equipment."

Natsumi's dark eyes glinted while one hand closed into a fist. She looked around at the group then down at the table.

"If we figure out who did this, that person is going to get in trouble with the school. They broke into a building and possibly vandalized East Rapids property. Whoever did this could get suspended. Maybe even *expelled.*"

The entire group was silent. This wasn't just playing cops and robbers. What they did in the League had consequences. They could get other people in big trouble, and if they messed up, they could get someone innocent in trouble, not to mention getting into trouble themselves.

John jumped in his chair as Malena knocked loudly on the table. Everyone looked at her.

"Whatever happens," she said, "somebody is going to get in a massive amount of trouble. Natsumi, remember when we created the League of Scientists? Do you remember what I told you?"

Natsumi nodded. "You said you wanted to do more. You wanted to make the world better."

"Yeah," Malena laughed. "And you said we should just start with East Rapids, our community."

Natsumi smiled and dipped her head. "You have to start somewhere."

"Look," Malena said. "No one gets through life without messing up. We could make a mistake. We could get some kid in trouble because of this ghost. But forget all that. There's something more important. *We are looking for the truth.* If we remember that one thing, we're good. Other people may hate us for it, and we might not like what happens. But at least we know we did the right thing."

Malena's eyes burned with a fiery passion as she paused to look each of her friends in the eye.

"So," she said, "we have a big decision to make right now. Every one of us. We're moving beyond broken streetlights." She smiled at John then turned back to the group. "This isn't just a science club—we're doing more than just experiments. The question is, do we want to? I want to know if you're in this. For real. If not, it's cool. But I need to know—right now—because we could fall pretty hard."

The four friends were nodding before Malena had even finished talking. Malena nodded back.

"Good."

"We could fall and land hard," Hector said. "Or we could bounce."

Malena laughed. "Cool. Then we continue."

"So what's next?" John asked.

In response, Malena pointed toward the closed door. "Okay. Kimmey and Natsumi, what are you hiding in there?"

"Wait!" Hector said. "What about the evil dihydrogen monoxide? I don't want to get infected with anything."

Natsumi tried to hold in a smile as she looked at Kimmey.

"Hector," Kimmey said. "That was just to keep you from getting in our way."

"I don't get it." He looked at Natsumi.

"Dihydrogen monoxide," she spoke quietly, biting back a grin, "is two hydrogen atoms bound to an oxygen atom. H_2O."

"So ... H_2O ..." Hector's struggle stopped as realization dawned. He looked at Natsumi in amazement.

"Yup," she said, smiling. "Dihydrogen monoxide is just water."

Hector whooped, jumped up, and sprang for the door.

CHAPTER 16

Malena was faster. She reached the door first and pushed Hector back.

"Hold on. Let Natsumi and Kimmey through. This is their project."

"You bet it is," Kimmey exclaimed. "We worked hard on this one."

"And we got to watch the TekMage movie, too," Natsumi said to Hector.

"TekMage? What does that have to do with—"

"Nothing," Kimmey interrupted. "We thought of all this entirely on our own."

Kimmey didn't smile, but Natsumi did. The others decided not to ask; instead, they squeezed past Hector and into the Lab.

It took them a minute to recognize it as their Lab. The desk, futon, and bookshelves had been hidden from view, shoved up against the wall and out of whatever sunlight managed to sneak its way around the windows taped over with black tarp. Though the overhead light was on, the room was gloomy.

Kimmey and Natsumi led the others to the center of the room where a folding table held some equipment.

"Here's what we've got," Kimmey said, poking a finger at the table. On it were two big, blue plastic tubs filled with water.

"Here's a water pump from my old fish tank," Kimmey said, lifting up the pump, "and we've got some plastic tubing. We'll use these to move water from one tray to the other."

"Hold on," Malena said. "Tell us why. I'd like to know what's going on first."

"Actually, it's pretty simple," Natsumi answered. "We had to try and create the 'ghost,' ourselves. If we could make a ghost, then someone else could, too."

John bit the inside of his cheek. "But Casey's story was so ... *weird.* Like from a movie. You can't make that happen in real life. Can you?"

"You just said a movie effects person could do it," Kimmey accused. "We figured we'd try, too. Hector, hit the lights."

He flipped the wall switch, and the room went almost completely dark. There was a quiet click.

Kimmey held a strange-looking flashlight under her chin. Her face lit up by an otherworldly, dark-purple glow. Her tanned skin was now barely visible. Kimmey smiled and her teeth glowed a bright white. Her eyes were frightening with thin rings of white surrounding large black circles.

"Hey, Kimmey," Hector said. "I never noticed how freaky your eyes are."

"There's a movie special effect for you," she said, laughing. She blinked slowly and dramatically at John.

"This is a black light." Her teeth vanished and reappeared as she spoke. "I wear contacts, and those make my eyes look even cooler. You should see what it's like when I take one contact out and leave the other in. I was playing in front of the mirror with the black light for about an hour."

Hector stepped closer to Kimmey and studied her. "You've got a bunch of tiny little white flecks all over your skin. Your clothes, too."

"It's dust. With a black light, you can see a lot of things you don't usually see."

"It's so cool how it makes things glow," Hector said, staring closely at Kimmey's teeth.

"Visible light wavelength and radiation," John said.

"Huh?"

"John's got it," Kimmey said. "There are different kinds of light. Regular light, infrared, ultraviolet. The sun gives off multiple kinds of light, and ultraviolet is the part of sunlight that gives you a sunburn if you stay outside too long. And when you turn out the regular lights and only turn on ultraviolet, the black light makes things look really cool. This is a light that's designed to shine ultraviolet light." She used one fingernail to tap the thick flashlight.

"Well, then don't point it at me!" Hector said.

"Relax. Don't freak out. This isn't the sun. It's just a little light with four batteries. Some black lights *can* be dangerous, but not this one because it has a safe wavelength. Think of it as something between a flashlight and a laser pointer."

"So what's it for?" Malena asked, sounding impatient.

"Some things," Kimmey said, "glow really bright under a black light like my teeth and Hector's shoelaces." She flicked the light quickly to shine on Hector's feet. He tried to jump out of the way. Rolling her eyes, Kimmey changed the subject. "Step one is the swirling fog and cold water."

Natsumi said, "Right. Like we planned, Kimmey. Let's show them."

"Stand back, everyone," Kimmey said, spreading her arms wide, "and check it out."

Kimmey got to work in the dark room, plugging various tubes into the water pump. She flicked a switch, and the pump started chugging quietly, taking water from one tub and streaming it into the other. Kimmey shined the black light at the tubs, and the water inside them stayed black.

"That's our model of the swimming pool," Natsumi said. She pulled on a pair of thick, rubber-gripped ski gloves. The stitching detail glowed a bright red in the black light. She leaned over and lifted up a thick, heavy paper bag. Even in the warm room, it had a layer of frost and ice on the outside. She opened it, reached in and pulled something out.

"Say hello to our ghostly fog."

Smoke poured from her fingers as she slowly opened her gloved hand. A few small chunks of ice rested on her palm. They glowed a bright white.

"Dry ice!" Hector said. He reached for Natsumi's hand, and she yanked it away with a puff of fog.

"Don't touch," she said. "That's frozen carbon dioxide. It's more than 100 degrees below zero Fahrenheit. You don't want to touch this stuff without gloves. It would burn your skin."

"Burn me? From ice?"

"Yes. Science is weird like that. You can get burned from something really cold."

She turned her hand over and dropped the dry ice into the tub of water. Almost immediately, a white, smoke-like haze appeared, slowly developing into a fog that floated just above the roiling water.

"The fog is caused by the dry ice," Natsumi said. "Dry ice is one of only a few things on Earth that doesn't melt. It just becomes a gas automatically. It's called 'sublimation.' Anyway, when we put the dry ice in water, it turns back into a gas and creates this fog. At the same time, it makes the water incredibly cold."

Hector squinted at the fog, watching it grow thick and heavy over the water. He thought he could see shapes in it. It was just like how Casey had described his ghost.

"Wow," Malena said. "I never thought about dry ice. Good thing you're a chemist, Natsumi."

Natsumi smiled shyly.

"How long will this stuff take to disappear?" John asked.

Natsumi thought for a moment. "It depends on the size. For what I used, maybe a couple minutes."

"So," John thought out loud, "Casey could have seen the fog and felt the cold water. Later, when the others came to the pool, the dry ice would have been long gone! Not a drop of evidence left to show anyone else."

Natsumi nodded at Kimmey. "That's what we thought, too."

"Next," Malena said, "the ghost."

"This part was harder," Natsumi said. "We needed to find something that could suddenly appear in the water and reach out for Casey."

"And glow!" Hector said.

"That took some research," Natsumi said. "We were online for a while, researching a bunch of different chemicals. There's actually a lot of options. And," she looked at Kimmey, "this is where the black light comes in."

"Right," Kimmey said. "Everyone, meet 'Baby Casey.'" She held a small plastic doll above her head.

"Cute," said Hector.

"It's not mine," Kimmey said quickly, lowering the doll. "It's my sister's. She hasn't played with this thing in years. I figured she wouldn't miss it while we ran some experiments."

"Yeah. Dr. Frankenstein said the same thing," Hector said.

Malena laughed as Kimmey put the doll in the tub. It floated on its back in the dark water and bounced along with the white fog.

"So," Kimmey said. "There's Casey in the cold, moving water. He's scared. He's wondering what's going on. Then ... Natsumi, are you ready?"

Natsumi nodded, pulled off her gloves and dropped them on the floor.

Kimmey shone the black light on the doll and the water around it. Natsumi did something to the other tub and the water pump, and then whispered a single word.

"*Boo.*"

A tentacle shot through the water, glowing a bright yellow-green in the black light. Malena watched eagerly, and John and Hector shouted as it appeared from the water pump. The glowing water headed toward the "swimmer," hit the doll, and began to spread. More and more of the yellow-green water surrounded the doll, and eventually the glow filled the entire tub.

"Our ghost," said Kimmey.

"What *is* that?" asked John. "Some kind of LED?"

"No. It's a special dye called 'fluorescein,' she said, pronouncing it *FLOOR-zeen.*

"Kimmey and I tried to find a glowing liquid, something that was safe to put in water. Fluorescein matched what we were looking for."

"How did you get it?" John said.

"Kimmey found a bunch of possible chemicals, and I narrowed it down to this one. I asked my mom to order it.

She checked it out and made sure it was safe for us to use. She actually uses something like it on her own patients; she puts it in eye drops that go into her patients so that she can find any problems. Fluorescein is super strong, though. You only need a little. I used a few drops just now, and *that* was way too much." She held up a small, white screw-top container. "This little bottle could easily turn a whole pool green."

"Green? *That's* not green," John said, pointing to shining drips of dark orange liquid drooling down from the top of the container.

"Before you mix it with water, fluorescein is actually orange."

John stepped back as Kimmey shoved her hand in front of John's face. She spread open her fingers. "It's hard to see in the black light, but my fingertips are orange. It disappears from water pretty fast, but it stains your skin. Even if you wash your hands."

Malena stared at her hands, "That's interesting. I wondered how you were going to make the ghost."

"What?!" Kimmey exclaimed, offended. "We come up with this cool solution, fog and a glowing ghost, and that's all we get out of you?"

"Plenty of things glow in nature," Malena said. "John and I learned about the anglerfish, but that's living bacteria making the glow. This isn't alive and wasn't something I could've guessed."

"Uh huh," said Kimmey, annoyed.

"What I'm trying to say," laughed Malena, "is nice job!"

"So that's it!" John said. "That's the ghost! That's what happened to Casey!"

Natsumi and Kimmey looked at each other. Kimmey shook her head.

Natsumi said, "Not exactly. This doesn't mean Casey's ghost doesn't exist. This is just one possible answer."

"But how can you see something like this," John pointed at the doll as it floated in the tub of glowing yellow-green water, "and still believe in ghosts?"

"Because this doesn't disprove ghosts."

"What?"

"It's like this," Kimmey said. "Say you wanted to make some fake blood."

"Okay," John said.

" Now, for *fake* blood, you could use ketchup or red paint or colored corn syrup. Which is the right way?"

"Any of them, I guess," John said.

"Okay, so I use ketchup. Does that mean real blood doesn't exist? Does it mean red paint and corn syrup don't exist?"

"No. Ketchup is just one way of making fake blood. The others are still possible." John paused. "Oh, I get it. A ghost could still exist. You just found one other explanation of what this ghost *might* be."

"That's all this is," Natsumi said quietly. "We collect the facts. Deduce the explanations. Then we see which one makes the most sense."

"Okay," Malena said, talking fast. Her eyes shone eerily in the black light. "One of us needs to talk to Coach Warren about this. Like you, Kimmey."

"The coach? What for?"

"We need to try this at full size. For real. Like at the swim meet."

Everyone stared at Malena.

"I've got an idea." She nodded to herself, excited. "We don't have much time, though, and we need to get ready. Kimmey, get the coach's permission to use the pool for a big test. Natsumi, can you get more dry ice? Like, a *lot* of it?"

"Probably," Natsumi said.

Malena whirled to look at Hector and John. "You saw what Natsumi and Kimmey did, how they created the 'ghost'?"

"Sure," Hector said.

"You get to do it, too. Only, this is going to be huge. Don't go anywhere. We need to talk."

Hector and John looked at each other.

"I guess I could talk to the coach tomorrow morning before class," Kimmey said. "We've only got a few more days before the swim meet on Tuesday. Let's meet back here tomorrow after school, and I'll let you know how it goes."

Hector shook his head. "Hey, guys, it's great we have a plan, but did anyone notice?" He pointed at Kimmey's black light. "We're not done here. You guys still missed something, something big."

Kimmey looked surprised. "We did?"

"Yeah," he spread his arms. "You forgot about the sun! We're in a dark room. You showed us this cool glowing dye. But it's dark in here, and we need a special flashlight to even see the glow! Casey swam in the pool in the morning with the sun shining. This is cool, but it doesn't match what happened. Also Casey didn't say the water was a yellowish-greenish color. He said it was *green*." He pointed at the glowing water.

As Hector talked, Natsumi walked over to the covered window. Kimmey was nodding patiently.

"You're right, Hector." She looked at Natsumi, and yelled, "Now!"

Kimmey clicked off the black light flashlight and the room was completely dark.

In one fast motion, Natsumi yanked the plastic tarp from off the window. Everyone squinted as sunlight streamed into the room.

John watched, amazed, as the water in the tub glowed a rich bright green. "What we wanted to save for last," Kimmey said, "was to show you how *fluorescein glows green in sunlight*."

"Oh," Hector said. "Now *that's* cool."

"Yeah," Malena said. Her big eyes shone with the reflected green glow. "It is."

CHAPTER 17

The next morning at school, John couldn't stop yawning. He hadn't slept well the previous night. He would roll over, squint at the clock and see that only five minutes had passed since the last time he'd checked. Then when he finally did get to sleep, he dreamed about waking up to check the clock.

Sleeping was hard work.

He had too much to worry about. The ghost mystery was pretty cool, though, and was a "problem" he was happy to have.

After seeing Natsumi's and Kimmey's ghost, Malena gave him a challenge: build a robot. The robot had to pour dry ice and liquid into a container of water all by itself. The container had to be big. It would, in fact, be the East Rapids swimming pool.

The League would use this robot to automatically mix the "ghost ingredients" into the pool. It was important that a robot do the work, Malena said, but she didn't say why.

John had some ideas and was working with Hector to build and test the robot. And, to make Hector happy, he even had a name for it: "Houdini."

Harry Houdini, the most famous magician and escape artist ever, was also one of the greatest ghost investigators. He never found a real ghost, but toured the world exposing frauds and fakes. Hector and John hoped their own electronic "Houdini" might do the same and would help them find the truth about Casey's ghost.

John loved thinking about the ghost mystery. It was exhilarating. He felt useful, important. Yet this importance came at a price: everything else in his life was falling apart.

He was behind on homework and hadn't been paying attention in either Mr. Steinhacker's or Ms. Heida's classes. His homework was routinely late, so he'd leave for school early to tell the teachers before classes started. He couldn't stand the humiliation of being yelled at in front of peers, so he got up extra early to make sure any yelling was done before class, not during.

It was weird how different the teachers had acted. Like usual, Mr. Steinhacker had gotten angry. His face hadn't turned bright red, though. It was just a medium-pink, so John knew it could've been worse. Before John left, Mr. Steinhacker had snapped, "Well, your work better be in to*morrow.*"

When John told Ms. Heida the same thing, she did something completely different. She looked at John, concerned, with her head tilted a little. Even without other students there,

John felt embarrassed. Then, instead of yelling at him or demanding the essay for the next day, she asked a question.

"Is everything okay, John?"

No, it isn't, John wanted to say. There was all the homework to do. That was enough pressure. There was the ghost mystery, which was awesome, but he still had to find time to investigate it and be with the League.

And, of course, there was Dowser. After yesterday's frantic chase through the neighborhood, John was more worried than ever. He didn't want to get beat up, and he didn't want to have to look at Dowser again. But Dowser would be there, leering at him during every class, "accidentally" slamming into him in the hallway. He was always, always there.

"Yes. Everything's fine," John said. He avoided her eyes. He knew she didn't believe him, but he couldn't tell her. She just wouldn't get it.

"John," Ms. Heida said, and something in her voice made him look up. She was smiling gently. "Just let me know if I can help with anything, all right? Anything. That's what teachers are for. As for the assignment, how much time do you need to finish it?"

"I don't know," John mumbled. "Like a day or so."

"Okay," Ms. Heida said. "Then get it to me tomorrow. Just this once, okay?"

"Okay."

That embarrassing conversation occurred before school. John figured the day would probably get worse. After all, Dowser was in John's first class, sitting at a table in the back of the room. John sat as far away as possible.

As the class began, John glanced at Dowser, trying to see if he was loading up a spit wad, a rubber band cannon, anything. He wasn't.

Weird, John thought, looking more carefully. *I guess I got lucky.*

"Mister Hawkins, I need you to pay *attention*!"

Oh, great.

Mr. Elinger was looking right at John. His face was red.

John sat forward and tried to pay attention, except when Mr. Elinger turned toward the board with his back to the class. Then John watched Dowser. Dowser usually attacked whenever the teacher turned away. John braced himself.

Nothing happened.

Dowser wasn't even looking at him. In fact … John did a double take just to make sure. Dowser was actually... *paying attention.* It was like he was possessed by the ghost of a good student.

Something weird was going on.

***

The rest of the day bounced between scary and boring. During class changes, John shot out of his chair and ran out of the room, looking over his shoulder at Dowser. Every time, his worry changed to confusion. Dowser never followed him.

John got more and more worried as the end of the school day came closer and closer. Dowser had chased him yesterday and would've pounded him if John hadn't escaped. Today would be worse. Dowser was probably saving himself up for an attack right after school ended; something John would have a hard time avoiding.

But even if he couldn't escape, he'd still try.

After his last class, John ran out and dove into a big group of students. Everyone was loud, yelling and laughing, and a lot of kids were pushing each other and playing around. John hunched down and stayed in the middle of the group. It was the perfect disguise.

The plan seemed to work. No Dowser.

John realized there was a problem. The mass of students was great cover, but it wouldn't stay that way. The cluster was already breaking apart. Some students headed toward the buses, some toward the bike racks, and others started to walk home.

In desperation, he stayed with the biggest group—the bus kids. They headed toward a long line of yellow school buses.

John always walked home. He couldn't get on a bus. He had no idea where it would go, but he stuck with the group as he frantically tried to think of a new plan.

John's camouflage began to disappear. He picked a bus at random, then followed some students who were heading toward that bus. Finding himself standing in front of the open door, looking at the dirty black stairs, he stopped. He knew he couldn't get in.

Suddenly, he stumbled forward as if someone had shoved him from behind. He landed hard on his knees and skinned his hands painfully on the concrete. Terrified, he knew who it was.

It's Dowser! he thought, panicking. *Get up get up get up!*

He scrambled around, moving fast, trying to decide whether to scream or run. He was already breathing so hard that he wasn't sure he could do either.

But it wasn't Dowser. It was a little girl, a head shorter than John, with long brown hair held back by a ladybug barrette. She stuck her tongue out at John, stepped around him, and jumped up the bus stairs. John, his heart racing, his hands and knees burning, just stared at her.

"On or off, kid?" The irritated bus driver looked at him. "You're holding up the line."

John stepped aside. His cover vanished as the mass of students climbed on the bus. John broke away and ran. He left as quickly as he could, but he still had a sinking feeling.

No matter how fast he moved, no matter where he went, Dowser was faster and would find him. But he was wrong. There was no Dowser for the entire run home.

It was so weird, John thought. The entire day he had worried about Dowser and nothing happened. He didn't know why, and in that moment he didn't care. He just wanted to go to his workshop and work on Houdini.

He was still running, but he relaxed a bit as he got closer to home. *At least for a day*, he thought, *things could get back to normal.*

Out of breath, John arrived at his house, his legs shaking and tired. He burst through the front door and then stopped and stared.

His mother stood beside the kitchen sink, still in the yellow shirt she wore for her job. She must've gotten off work early today. When John burst through the door, she whipped her head around, short brown hair flying back. Concern instantly filled her face. "Are you all right?"

"He's just fine," a man said, lifting himself from his seat at the kitchen table. He walked over to John. He stuck out his hand for a handshake.

It was the old man from yesterday. This time, he wasn't threatening John with a flyswatter, but John still recognized him.

"What are you doing here? Am I in trouble?"

The man and his mom smiled at his question, but it didn't make him feel any better. Why was this man in his house, talking to his mom? How in the world had the man found him?

He had no answers. But he knew one thing for sure: Things were *not* back to normal.

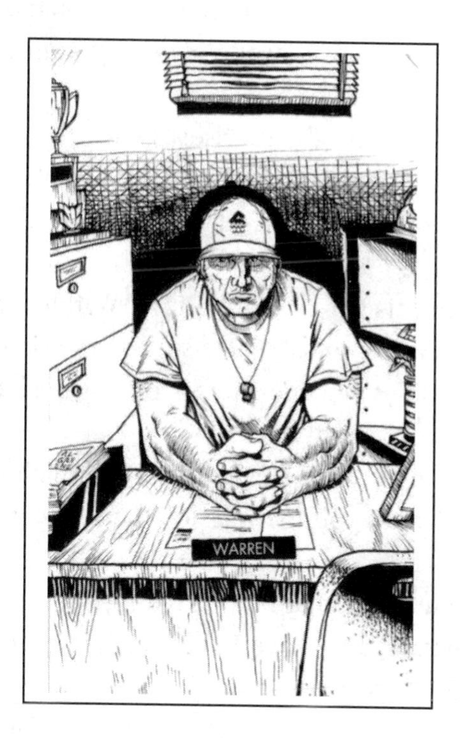

CHAPTER 18

After school let out, Kimmey stayed late. She headed to the ground floor and stopped in front of Coach Warren's door. She smoothed a wisp of hair from her face and knocked.

"Come in."

Kimmey opened the office door and was immediately hit by the smell of chlorine and mildew. It was not pleasant. Even worse, the smell was trapped in the tiny room. It looked like a converted closet with barely enough space for a desk, chair, and filing cabinet. Kimmey leaned into the room to look around.

"You're looking for the broom and mop, aren't you?" Coach Warren laughed. "I had to throw those away to make room so I could sit down!"

He pushed away from his desk, and the back of his chair bumped against the opposite wall. "Kimmey, right? What can I do for you?"

"I need to talk to you about Casey's ghost."

His smile sagged, then turned rueful. "Again? You're probably the hundredth student who's asked me about this."

"Really?"

"You sure are. 'Is Casey in trouble?' 'Will he swim in the meet?' 'Was it *really* a ghost?'" He smiled and shook his head. "Everyone's got the same questions. Come on, ask me something I haven't heard!"

"Well," Kimmey began, hesitating. Then, with a sideways grin, she said, "I want your permission to use the pool to make another ghost."

The coach burst out laughing. "Finally," he said, "I gotta say, I haven't heard that one yet!" He laughed again. "Is that a serious question?"

"Yeah. If we can make a ghost like the one Casey saw, then there may not *be* a ghost. If we can duplicate it, we might be able to calm everyone down."

"I don't think that's a good idea," Coach Warren said. The lines around his mouth grew taut, his lips set in a firm line. When he spoke next, his voice was deep and authoritative. "The swim meet is coming up soon," he said. "The team needs time to practice. I can't have them distracted."

"We'd like to do it at the meet. Right before it starts. See, we could scare out whoever—"

He snorted. "No. You're not gonna do that. Not to my team. The students are already worried about Casey. I'm not going to hurt our chances even more with a stunt like that. The ghost isn't even a big deal anymore. Everyone's already forgotten about it."

"You said a hundred students talked to you about this!" Kimmey exclaimed, indignant.

The coach banged his hand on the top of his desk. "No more ghost talk, and no chemistry experiments in my pool. Am I understood?" His steely blue eyes did not leave her face. Kimmey felt herself shrinking beneath them.

She turned to go, her face burning. Her hair fell out of place, and she pushed it away angrily. She had barely taken two steps out of Coach Warren's office before he slammed the door behind her.

Kimmey stalked away. As she thought about what happened, something occurred to her. She stopped walking.

I never mentioned a chemistry experiment. How did he know that's what it was?

CHAPTER 19

Armed with new suspicions, Kimmey knew she needed to push Coach Warren a little harder, either to prove his innocence or to expose his guilt. This would be tricky, though. She wasn't on any of Coach Warren's teams, but she could still get in trouble with him if she pushed too hard. The trick was to lighten the load by getting someone else to help her push.

She still had time. Most of the students had left the school, but teachers usually stayed late. Kimmey jogged up to Ms. Heida's room.

Out of all the teachers in the school, Kimmey liked Ms. Heida the best. She was cool and a good teacher. She didn't need to be strict or yell at anyone in class. She kept things moving too quickly for anyone to mess around.

Now, the classroom was silent. Ms. Heida was alone at her desk, typing on her computer. Kimmey knocked on the open door and walked in.

"Excuse me, Ms. Heida?"

"Hi, Kimmey. What's up?"

"I need help. Do you have a minute?"

Ms. Heida listened as Kimmey explained what the League had been doing and their hypothesis about Casey's "ghost."

"Please don't tell anyone about the League," Kimmey added when she'd finished. We're trying to keep it secret for now."

"Really?" Ms. Heida said. "It seems to me you'd be able to get more done if you *weren't* so secretive. Besides, if you want more cases, you'll have to tell people about the League, won't you?"

"I guess so," Kimmey said. "I know that Hector set up a website, but we haven't told anyone about it. Besides, we want to keep the membership a secret."

"If you have a website and investigate mysteries for people, won't you have to meet them?"

"Yeah. Probably. Maybe." Kimmey had never thought about that. Could they really stay hidden, and should they? "It just seems cooler to be secretive, I guess. Like we're doing something really important," Kimmey confessed.

Ms. Heida laughed. "You're smart. You'll figure something out."

Kimmey thought a moment, her pretty blue eyes bright. Then she said, "We don't want our mystery solving to be motivated by anything other than goodwill and trust in science. It's not supposed to be a popularity contest, not for us."

Ms. Heida smiled. "I think this 'League of Scientists' is a great idea. If you need help or advice, let me know." She paused, then added seriously, "I'm sure Coach Warren doesn't know anything more about this 'ghost' than anyone else, but I'll go speak with him. And Principal Murray, too."

"Wow, thanks!" Kimmey said, surprised.

"Tell you what," Ms. Heida said. "I'll go and talk to them now. Pop in tomorrow, and we'll talk some more, okay?"

"Sure," Kimmey said. Ms. Heida stood up, and together, they both left the room. Ms. Heida turned right, and Kimmey turned left, as though she were going to leave. Kimmey only made it to the next classroom, however, before she slipped inside. Peeking her head around the door, she watched Ms. Heida walk away.

Kimmey didn't want to hear what happened tomorrow. She wanted to know right now.

CHAPTER 20

"How do you know who I am?" John said. "How did you find me?"

The man smiled, which deepened the lines around his mouth.

"Now, John," his mom said, "Be polite. I believe you know this gentleman, Mr. Watson." She stood beside the sink, hands on her hips nervously. Her face looked too long against her bobbed brown hair, and the bags under her eyes had suddenly become prominent. John thought that his mother looked very, very tired.

They shook hands. Mr. Watson's skin was dry and scratchy. John pulled away and looked at his mom.

"What's going on?"

His mom bit her lip. "Mr. Watson and I have been talking. He told me about yesterday, about what happened with you and Brandon."

"Who?"

"Brandon LaMange."

"Oh. Dowser."

John's mom shook her head. "Who?"

"It's my name for Brandon. Because he's always dowsing, you know? Like he thinks he knows what's going on, but he's always just completely wrong."

"What's dowsing?"

"When you try to find underground water with a stick ..." Seeing his mother's expression, John stopped. "Never mind."

"John—"

"Nothing happened, Mom. Honest!"

"I know that, honey." She pressed her lips together and got a look on her face. It was a look that meant she was thinking about something very serious and emotional and that she was going to talk for a long time. John hated that look.

"Ms. Hawkins," Mr. Watson said. "May I interrupt?"

She began to reply, then closed her mouth and nodded.

"With all due respect," Mr. Watson began, "I was there. I saw it. I videoed the damage done to my yard." John started to protest, and the man held up a thick hand. "Not you. This LaMange kid. Don't worry, I got the whole thing."

"How?" John said.

The man reached into his pocket and pulled out a flat black box. He pressed a button, and John heard a faint click. The box separated and slid open, revealing a small screen. The screen flickered, then turned a dark blue.

"Look familiar?" Mr. Watson asked.

He pressed another button and held the screen up to John's face. It began playing a video. Amazed at the tiny device, John watched himself run into Mr. Watson's backyard. The movie looked like it was from a camera mounted somewhere high on Mr. Watson's house. The John on the tiny screen looked around desperately, then ran forward and grew bigger before disappearing from sight underneath the camera.

Mr. Watson's hand twitched one way and the screen went black. Another twitch and the black box slid shut with another quiet click.

"You got ... everything?" John said.

"Yeah," Mr. Watson said. "You. LaMange. And remember, I was there, too."

"I remember. I thought you were going to swat me!"

"Nah," Mr. Watson said, waving a hand. "You were safe. I don't even like swatting flies."

John's mom spoke up. "Mr. Watson is here to talk about the bullying, John. It needs to stop."

"No, Mom! If you get Dowser in trouble, he'll just come after me!"

"No, honey, he won't. I'll call his parents. Maybe I'll talk to your teachers, too."

She said more, but John stopped listening. This was bad. If Dowser got in trouble because of him, the bullying would just get worse.

"Excuse me again," Mr. Watson said. "But just leave it. Don't do anything."

"I'm sorry?" John's mom said.

"A question, John," Mr. Watson said. "How was school today?"

"Fine."

"That's what he says every day," his mom said. "Something happened, didn't it?" She was getting worked up again.

"No, Mom," John said. "Nothing happened today, really! Dowser never even looked at me. I swear. It worried me because I thought he was going to ..."

John trailed off and looked at Mr. Watson. The old man stood there, grinning. He rocked back on his heels and nodded.

"Remember what I said? If life goes straight, you go sideways. That's what I did. I checked my security camera. I spoke with Brandon."

"You *what*?!" John exclaimed. "Why? What did you say?"

Mr. Watson laughed. "It's all right. He and I, we understand each other. I just explained a few things, and made it clear: If he wanted to stay happy, then he would need to leave you alone."

"What does that mean?"

"John. Remember what else I told you? I know what it's like to be bullied. I've been there. I also know that you're never stuck. There's always a way out. And I know that you don't want help, but I helped anyway. I don't think you'll have to worry about Brandon anymore."

John shook his head, confused.

Mr. Watson continued. "I used my brain, John. I have this 'Dowser' kid—Brandon—on video, damaging my yard. So, now we have a deal. He leaves you alone, and I won't ask for yard repairs or talk to his parents about what I saw."

John thought back to the broken streetlight. The League solved the mystery and stopped the student from breaking it again. No one had gotten hurt.

"Really?" John said.

"John," Mr. Watson said, still looking at him. "You said nothing happened today. Verify some more. All you have to do is wait. If things get worse, then I'm wrong. I'll apologize, and I'll work with your mother to make things right. But I don't think any of that will happen."

"Today *was* weird," John said. "Dowser ... he never even looked at me!"

Mr. Watson's eyes were sharp. "If you're smart, then you're strong," he said. He tapped the side of his head with his small black box.

John looked at the tiny video player. "What is that thing? I only saw one button. How did you make it work?"

"I can't tell *all* my secrets! Knowledge is power, right?" He laughed, shook his head, and quickly slipped the black box into his pocket. "Let's see how the next week goes. Then, if your mom's okay with it, I'll show you some of my toys. You like electronics? You like making things?"

John nodded.

"You'll love my setup. I've got motion detectors, streaming video, Internet bots spidering photo archives, facial detection and feature comparison software, WHOIS...well, it's interesting stuff. It's how I found you and your buddy, Brandon."

"Really?"

"I live close to your school, so I figured you were both students. I got you on video and then ran a special program that compared your faces with any local photos it could find online. I got a big list of websites where the program thought it saw you. All I had to do was look at a few, find your face and see what the page was about. I found Dowser right away—he's not careful. He posted plenty of pictures of himself online for anyone to see. Tracking him was simple."

John's mom looked worried. "Pictures like that shouldn't be online. John, I told you not to share pictures—"

"He didn't," Mr. Watson said. "John was tough to find. I eventually found one picture from a few weeks ago. It was a scanned photo showing all the students in the East Rapids LabTech science club. John didn't post it. Another LabTech student did."

“That’s cool!” John said.

Mr. Watson shrugged. “I suppose. It’s just what I do. Or it’s what I used to do. Government stuff. I’m retired now. I spend almost as much time on the plants in my backyard.” He laughed. “Those are interesting, too.”

“What?” John’s head was spinning. “I don’t get it. I mean, you used all these things to find Dowser and me. How did you get all this equipment?”

Mr. Watson shook his head. He lifted his hand and looked down at the tiny, black video player.

“Nah. I didn’t get them from anywhere. My toys aren’t at any store. I built them.”

John smiled. He thought of the Houdini device he planned to make to recreate Casey’s ghost. “Do you think you could help me with a project? I need to build something, too.”

Mr. Watson smiled. “I’d love to.”

CHAPTER 21

Natsumi watched as the Lab's front door slowly opened. Seeing John stumble backward through the door, she ran to help. He was struggling to carry a huge metal bucket in both arms. It looked heavy. Hector came in behind John, his hands in his pockets.

"What *is* that thing?" Malena said.

John looked hurt. "It's what you wanted us to make. It's Houdini!" He slowly advanced to stand beside the table. Panting, he nodded to Natsumi, and they placed it down together.

Hector watched eagerly as John carefully slid the contraption to the center of the table. The metal on metal contact screeched loudly, and everyone winced.

"You're going to love this!" Hector said. "Meet the very first 'Fluorescein-Ultra-Dynamic-Dispersal-Unit!"

"So, it's called 'FUDDU'?!" Malena laughed. Natsumi smiled.

"Yeah. FUDDU. That was my name for it," Hector said.

John muttered, "I like 'Houdini' better."

"Okay, okay," Malena said through her laughter. "Houdini."

As the group gathered around the device, Hector looked around. "Where's Kimmey? She'd probably pound us if we worked without her!"

"I don't know," Malena said. "Anyone see her in school today?"

"I did," John said.

"So did I," Natsumi said. "Maybe she had to do something at home."

"Well, yeah," Malena said. "But her house is, like, a hundred feet away. Even if she had to be at home, she'd stop here first. She must still be at school."

John had a vision of Dowser stalking Kimmey and swallowed.

Hector caught the look.

"¿Qué pasó, amigo?" he asked.

"Well," John said slowly. "Dowser tried to beat me up the other day—"

"What?!" Malena cried.

John looked at her, and the burning in her eyes scared him more than Dowser ever had.

"No! It's okay!" John said. "Nothing happened. I hid in some guy's house!"

"What?!"

John's face was red. He didn't answer.

"Look. John. If this stuff happens, you've got to tell someone. Like, well, *us*. Right? We've got your back. We're your friends."

John stared down at the table.

Hector tried to break the tension. "Well, in that case, can the League help *me*? I got beat up once when I was in second grade. Aaron Connor sat on me and called me a booger."

John snorted a laugh.

"Hector!" Malena said. She sounded angry, but her eyes smiled.

"What I wanted to say," John said, looking around at his friends, "is that I made a new friend. His name is Mr. Watson, and he helped me make Houdini. Plus, I think he solved the Dowser problem—for now, at least."

"How?" Natsumi asked.

"Tell us later," Malena said. Somehow, John wasn't offended by her interruption. She was kind and he knew that she still cared. "Not that it's not important, it's just that there are other things we need to discuss right now, like all these fantastic new devices!"

Natsumi smiled and then shook the big silver bucket sitting on the table. "So, what *is* this thing, guys?"

Hector gestured to John. John nodded and started to take things out of the bucket.

"Malena wanted Hector and me to make something that could dump a bunch of dry ice and fluorescein into the pool. Right?"

"Exactly," agreed Malena.

"But we needed a way to put it into the pool without anyone else seeing it happen. So, Houdini here is a remote controlled robot. We can operate him from hundreds of feet away."

"Him?' Not 'her?'" Malena said.

John looked uncomfortable. "Well, I just thought—"

Hector spoke up. "Houdini was a guy, Malena. The magician. The ghost hunter."

"Yeah," Malena said. "But his wife, Bess, kept on ghost hunting after he died."

"Really?" Hector said. "I didn't know that. Cool."

"Anyway," John said. "What we made was pretty simple. It was easy to figure out once I went to the pool and stuck my head in the maintenance room. The pool water goes through this big machine. I guess it cleans the water and adds chemicals and stuff. There's a part of the plumbing where you can open up a cover and see the water sitting in a tank right before it gets pumped into the pool."

"You did more than stick your head in the room," Hector said. "Were you supposed to be in there?"

"It was, like, thirty seconds. Honest. Anyway, since the water system is open right there, I figured what we needed was something like a giant bowl with a trap door on the bottom."

John lifted up the bucket, and awkwardly pointed the open end at Natsumi and Malena. There was a large silver hinge over half of the bucket's bottom and a small cup attached to the inside.

John hoisted the bucket to the side and held it between one arm and his hip. "You pour the fluorescein into the little cup here, and then you pile up dry ice all around it, but not so close that it freezes the fluorescein. Then you take it to the pool and mount it right above the tank in the maintenance room."

"Can I do the next part?" Hector asked eagerly.

"Sure."

"Okay," Hector said. "So, it's all ready. All in place, right? Then you get the remote control." He picked up a small black box and waved it.

"Then, when you're ready ..." He pressed a button on the remote. With a clunk, the bottom of the bucket rotated on a hinge and pointed down. "Anything inside the bucket falls through. Anything inside the cup pours out."

"Voilá!" John said. "The ghost is in the water!"

Malena looked deep in thought.

"This should work."

"Should?" Hector exclaimed. "That's all we get? You know how long it took to put this together?"

Malena blinked, then looked at Hector. "No. How long?"

"Well ..." Hector trailed off. "Actually, John did most of the work."

John nodded. "Mr. Watson, too, though. It took longer to plan it and find the right parts than to put it together. I had to cut out the bottom of the bucket and then reattach it by screwing on a hinge and the cup to hold the fluorescein. There's a little actuator arm with a battery pack. That's what the remote control talks to, so the bucket bottom can open and close. And since, you know, I have to go to school and stuff, it took a few days to get it all working right."

"Awesome, John," Malena said.

He smiled. "Thanks!"

Hector cleared his throat. "I gave him the batteries for the remote control."

Malena laughed. "Wow, that's hard work."

"Thanks!"

Malena looked around at everyone. "We're ready for action. Now, we just need permission to actually *do* this."

Everyone whirled as the front door slammed open, and Kimmey burst in. She was red-faced and out of breath.

"Guys!" She didn't even notice Houdini sitting on the table. "You're not going to believe this!"

Almost in one breath, Kimmey told the others about her run-in with Coach Warren and her visit to Ms. Heida.

"Then, when I followed Ms. Heida down the hallway, she went right to Coach Warren's office."

"Didn't she see you?" John asked.

"Nope. I kept out of sight. Like a seventh grade ninja."

"I don't think I could do that," John said. "What would you do if she caught you?"

"Caught me doing what? I'm a student at the school!"

Malena's eyes were bright. "So, Ms. Heida went into Coach Warren's office—"

"And she came out fast," Kimmey said. "She was in there for fewer than two minutes."

"How do you know? Did you count?" Hector asked.

"You're being obnoxious," Kimmey snapped. While Hector laughed, Kimmey turned to the rest of the gang and continued, "She came out, and she looked the same as I felt. Kinda frustrated. I kept following her, and she went to Principal Murray's office. I didn't go in. Mr. Geron is always in there, and I didn't want anyone to see me. Ms. Heida was in there a lot longer. I had to meet you guys—I was almost about to leave when she came out."

Natsumi said, "If she stayed in there that long, it was important."

"So what happened?" Hector asked.

"Ms. Heida saw me when she came back out. She didn't even seem surprised I was waiting there. She told me she talked with Principal Murray and Coach Warren. Here's where it gets weird: Ms. Heida said that the coach still doesn't want us to do anything at the swim meet."

John's shoulders slumped. "Really?" he asked. "All that work. I thought we could—"Hector asked, "Do you think he might have something to do with the ghost?"

Kimmey met his gaze. Hesitating, she finally said, "I think … it's possible."

"But why would he do something like that?" John cut in.

"I heard he's Kyle VanderJack's uncle. Maybe he really wants the West Shore team to win," Hector said.

"But won't that hurt his coaching career?" John said. "Isn't it in his best interest for our team to win?"

"Some family ties are really strong," Kimmey said.

"Wait," Malena said, interrupting. "Let's not assume anything until we know everything. Kimmey, what did Principal Murray say?"

Kimmey smiled. "It's on."

"Really?" John said. "We can do it?"

Kimmey was nodding. "Yeah. We can."

"Sweet!"

Natsumi said, "It's strange, though. Why would Principal Murray go over Coach Warren? Even if our plan works perfectly, we still might mess up the swim meet."

"I don't think so," Malena said. "We're just going to run an experiment right at the beginning before anyone's even in the water. It's got to be when a lot of people are watching. We need coaches and both swim teams to be there. After we're done, they can start swimming."

"In green water?" John asked, looking at Natsumi.

"No," Natsumi shook her head. "Fluorescein is biodegradable."

"Yeah," said Hector, "but we need something ultra bio-degradable."

"It is," Natsumi said. "If you leave it alone, the chemical bonds break down and quickly degrade into the environment. Chlorine actually accelerates the effect."

"So, the water won't be green for very long?" John asked Natsumi.

"Right."

"Know what I think?" Kimmey said. "We won't get in trouble. I mean, the *principal* said it was okay. I just hope he won't warn other people about it."

"He better not!" Malena said.

"Why not?" John questioned.

"For my plan, this has to be a surprise." She blew out a big breath and continued. "Okay. This is it, everyone. Let's figure out what's going to happen. I want to make sure that when our ghost appears, we all know what to do. Kimmey and Natsumi, you make sure we've got plenty of dry ice and fluorescein. Hector, do we still have the League of Scientists' website?"

"Yeah, it's out there—'www.LeagueOfScientists.com.' I haven't checked it in a while though."

"I don't get it," John said. "Don't we want to keep the League a secret?"

"No," Malena laughed. "We want to keep the membership—the five of us—a secret, but we want people to know about the League so we can get new mysteries to investigate. I figure the perfect way to do that is to be online. We can do cool stuff to help people, stay anonymous, and still feel like spies out of a movie!"

"So, we're staying anonymous just to feel cool?" John asked.

Malena lowered her eyebrows over her dark eyes and thought a moment. "No, I think it's more like a psychological thing. It makes it feel more legit, in a way."

"More legit?" Hector interrupted. Then he laughed. "It makes me feel sketchy, and that's why I love it!" He paused, catching the serious look on John's face, and added, "I'm kidding, by the way."

Malena laughed. “It makes me feel like I’m doing these things for the right reason. Not to be popular or cool, but because I love science and I love the truth.”

Natsumi clapped, her face bright.

Kimmey wiped away an imaginary tear. “So inspirational!”

Malena just grinned at her friends. “Back to business,” she turned to Hector. “Make sure the website’s still working,” she said. “Then show me how to see if anyone’s contacted us. After all this is over, people might want to reach us.”

“You got it.”

Malena turned to look at the equipment sitting on the kitchen table.

“John?”

“Yeah?”

“Get Houdini ready for magic.”

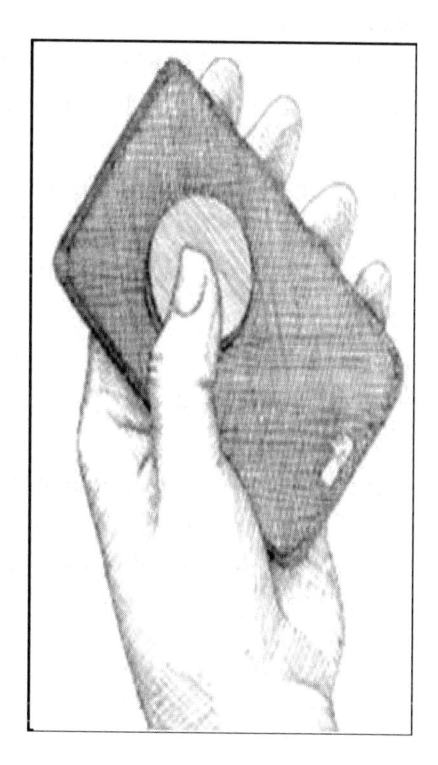

CHAPTER 22

The swim meet had a greater turnout than usual. School rivalry always drew crowds. For this meet, though, it looked like every student, from both East Rapids and West Shore, was there, and that they had all invited everyone they knew.

With all the commotion, no one noticed John step out of the pool maintenance room and into the main swimming area. The transmitter was heavy in his pocket. He stopped for a moment and breathed deeply through a wave of nausea. His hands were sweaty, and his heart pounded.

Yeah, he thought, *that'd be perfect, to throw up in front of a thousand people.*

He looked up at the stands where long metal bleachers spanned each side of the wide pool. They contained a noisy, jam-packed, constantly moving group of students, parents, and teachers.

John wanted to cover his ears. With no curtains or rugs to absorb sound, the yells and cheers bounced easily off the water, tiles and cement. He felt trapped inside an echo chamber that was getting louder by the minute.

He walked toward the side of the stands, trying to stay low. He hoped that if he hunched enough, people wouldn't notice him.

Houdini was ready. Back in the maintenance closet, John had mounted the big bucket in place. The bucket held a bunch of dry ice surrounding a small cup full of fluorescein. When he activated the transmitter, the bottom of the bucket would open and rotate down, dropping everything into the pool's water pump system.

"Hey there," called Hector, walking up to John from the locker rooms. A cell phone bulged against the pocket of his dark jeans. Hector was one of the few League members with a cell phone. At that moment, John was thankful. Walkie-talkies would have been too loud and too obvious. "Is this the place with the ghost?"

"Not so loud!" John said.

"Are you kidding?" Hector pointed up into the stands. "No one can hear us, even if we screamed at each other. Even if they did hear, they wouldn't care."

"They'd care," John said. "Everyone's still talking about the ghost."

"After today, they're going to be talking about it a *lot* more!" Hector grinned, then looked carefully at John. "Hey, come on, this is supposed to be fun! Are you okay?"

"Actually, I feel sick. Everyone's watching us."

Hector rolled his eyes. "No, they're not. Watch." Hector jumped up and down and waved to the audience with both arms. John, embarrassed, edged away. In response, a few people laughed and cheered.

"See," said Hector. "Hardly anyone cares!"

"*Now* they do," John grumbled. He glanced around nervously. "Can we just get off to the side? We should check the equipment again."

"It works. Don't worry. We tested this over and over. What's the worst that could happen?"

John didn't answer. Instead, he scanned the audience.

Oh no.

Dowser was there. He'd taken a seat far in the back, but John saw him. Unlike everyone else, Dowser *was* looking at John. The strange expression on his face was anger mixed with something else John couldn't figure out.

Their eyes met, but Dowser's expression didn't change. He just stared, his eyes flat. John looked away quickly.

Hector's phone rang. He answered it, and John could hear Malena's determined voice crackling through it. "We're in position. You should be, too," she said.

Hector looked around and saw Malena, Natsumi and Kimmey on the far side of the pool. He waved. Jerking his head to the left, he led John across from their friends. They quickly blended in with the swarming crowd next to the bleachers.

"Moving to our spot now."

"Good. We'll be here. Don't forget the plan."

Malena's instructions were simple: get in place so every member of the League could see as much of the bleachers and audience as possible. Then John would activate Houdini. There was time— right now—before the warm ups would start and students got in the pool.

The final step in Malena's plan was the easiest: watch what happened.

John tried to ignore the funny feeling in his stomach and turned his back on Dowser's strange glare. He focused. He didn't want to let anyone down.

After a couple moments of silence, Malena finally spoke again. "Tell John to start Houdini. It's time the world met our ghost!"

Hector glanced over at John, dark eyes sparkling excitedly. "You get that?"

John nodded and swallowed. He pulled Houdini's transmitter out of his pocket, thumbed on the power switch, and took a deep, shaking breath. Hector met his gaze. It was time.

"Do it."

Holding his breath, John slowly squeezed the button.

He visualized what was happening: at the speed of light, radio waves were blasting from his transmitter to Houdini's receiver. The bottom of the Houdini robot was opening up and pouring dry ice and fluorescein into the pool's water system. Powerful pumps were sucking in the ghostly water, pouring the bright, green and glowing water out into the pool. In fact, John realized, the ghost should be arriving right ... about ... *now.*

John felt a flood of relief. Whatever happened next, his job was done.

Nothing happened.

After a few more seconds, John's stomach dropped.

"Hector," John said. "Something's wrong! The ghost should be here by now!"

Hector searched the water. "Where is it? Is Houdini broken?"

John shook his head. "No way."

"Guys!" Malena's voice called nervously over the phone, "Did you release the ghost? Talk to me!"

2
4

Hector looked at John questioningly, the phone loose in his grasp.

John's hands trembled as he fumbled with the transmitter. "I don't know. I don't know, we tested everything! It *can't* be broken!"

He turned the small black box over in shaking hands, then stared at it.

"Oh, no. I don't believe this."

"What?" Hector said.

John pointed to the bottom of the transmitter.

"See that little red light glowing?"

"No."

"Neither do I." John looked at Hector, panicked. "That light glows when the transmitter's turned on. We tested everything over and over. It was too much. I think the batteries are toast."

Hector's mouth dropped. "You ... you put in dead batteries? It was working fine before."

"No! Well, maybe. I don't know. Maybe I forgot to turn the thing off. Wait—didn't *you* give me the batteries?"

"Well," Hector said quickly, "it doesn't really matter who, does it?"

John frantically opened the back of the transmitter and popped out two batteries. He clutched them tightly, then stopped, horrified.

"I didn't bring any spares!"

"I didn't either," Hector said. "We're in trouble."

Seeing that there was no relief in sight, John turned to Hector, his eyes wide and worried. "I'm sorry! I didn't think we'd—"

Hector sucked in a breath through his teeth. "Uh oh. We're out of time."

A group of swimmers stood at the edge of the pool, getting ready to jump in and warm up.

"Guys," Malena said, her voice crackling over the phone. "Have you released it?" She sounded nervous.

John felt tears in his eyes. The entire League of Scientists had counted on him, and he'd messed everything up with a stupid mistake. The ghost, Houdini, getting special permission from the principal, his chance to prove himself to his new friends, even his mom and Mr. Watson—everything was ruined because of him.

If Houdini didn't work—right *now*—he'd never forgive himself. But he was stuck, terrified. He couldn't move. It felt like when he hid behind Mr. Watson's funny-smelling couch.

In a flash, he remembered what Mr. Watson had said. *There was always a solution. The trick was to find it.*

"If life goes straight, you go sideways," he murmured, thinking furiously.

"What?" Hector said.

The camera! John had brought it along to take pictures of the ghost in the water, but now he thought that wasn't going to be necessary.

"Take this!" he exclaimed, and thrust Houdini's transmitter into Hector's hands. He tugged the camera from his pocket. It was his mom's old one, bulky and silver. It was the kind that still took batteries. He had only seconds.

Tearing at the battery compartment of the camera, John could hear Malena's voice coming through Hector's cell phone. "It's too late, guys! We should stop—"

"No!" John yanked out the batteries and wrenched the transmitter from Hector' grasp.

John slammed the batteries into place. He yelled as he saw the tiny LED glow a bright, strong red. He pressed the transmitter button.

It worked!

Three swimmers dived into the water.

Oh, no. No! No! No!

John didn't want to watch, but he couldn't look away. He stared at the swimmers, his heart hammering.

The ghost exploded into the water.

There was a moment's silence… then the screams began.

CHAPTER 23

As Malena watched, her mouth dropped open. This was all wrong. She expected the Houdini robot would slowly—*slowly!*—feed the fluorescein and dry ice into the pool's water supply. Houdini had worked, but not like it was supposed to. There was no fog. Instead, massive amounts of fluorescein flooded into the pool.

This was no single ghost acting alone, but a haunted family reunion. Multiple tentacles streamed out of every water jet in the pool. In the morning sun, the tendrils shone a bright, alien green. It looked as if a giant octopus was reaching for the unlucky swimmers. All of them were screaming and swimming frantically in different directions.

More glowing water sprayed into the pool and the tentacled hand looked as if it were squeezing. It closed in on the swimmers.

Malena shook her head slowly, marveling at the sight. Then her stomach lurched as she heard a deep rumbling noise. The floor shook under her feet.

The dry ice. It's coming.

She realized that the fluorescein must have hit the pool first because the thick liquid mixed so quickly with water. The dry ice took longer—it was a solid and needed time to sublimate. Their timing had been way off.

Malena knew dry ice was dangerous. It was terribly cold, of course, but there was also the pressure. Since gas takes up more space than ice, a balloon filled with melting dry ice crystals would grow and grow and eventually explode. She hoped the pool's water pipes were strong enough to keep from blowing up.

The rumbling grew louder.

Without warning, the pool's water jets hissed loudly, then violently sprayed white. A gentle fog slowly lifted its way above the water. It was mesmerizing—magical almost—to see the ghostly shapes appear right before their eyes.

The swimmers redoubled their efforts to escape. They swam fast through the body of the gigantic ghost, through glowing water and freezing fog. They struggled out of the pool. Green water streamed from their bodies and spattered on the floor as they ran, leaving glowing trails behind them.

***

Kimmey ignored the screams. It was tough—everyone in the building was making a lot of noise, and her ears were ringing. Things had gone really wrong. This wasn't supposed to happen, not like this.

With a feeling of dread, she thought about the simple experiment she and Natsumi had shown the others at the Lab. They had made a huge mistake: *a small experiment doesn't work the same as a big one*. When they made the experiment bigger, they made it much more complicated. More dangerous.

Kimmey saw Malena staring at the pool and Natsumi staring at Malena. Neither one paid attention to her.

It's up to me.

As desperate as she was to see what was happening, Kimmey turned away from the pool. She watched the audience.

Everyone, of course, was either yelling or panicking. Many students had jumped up and were running toward the pool, getting in the way of the escaping swimmers.

Well, *almost* everyone was panicking. In the West Shore section, she scanned the crowd for a student whose face matched the printout that was folded carefully in her pocket. It was the one Malena wanted them to keep an eye on.

She found him.

Kyle VanderJack.

Unlike everyone else, Kyle *wasn't* yelling, screaming his head off or pointing frantically at the pool. He stood near his teammates, dressed in warm up clothes. He faced the eerie water, but his eyes were out of focus. He looked dazed.

Kimmey walked over to him. "Hi, Kyle?"

He couldn't hear her over the background noise. She had to yell.

"*Kyle!*"

He turned his head toward her, but continued to stare at the pool. Then he blinked and dragged his eyes to hers.

"Yeah?" he yelled back.

Kimmey offered to shake hands. Without thinking, Kyle stretched out his own hand and shook. His eyes grew big when he realized Kimmey wasn't going to let go.

"Hey!" He tried to pull away, but Kimmey held on tightly.

She gave a sharp yank. Kyle stumbled toward her. As he fell forward, she locked her fingers around his wrist. He yelled as she pulled up his hand and looked at it closely.

Kyle's fingertips were stained orange.

"I've seen this before." She lifted up her other hand and showed Kyle her own fingers, stained an identical orange. "You've been playing with fluorescein, haven't you?"

Kyle, shocked, stared at her hand and then searched her face.

Kimmey grinned and spoke over the noise, "It's good to finally meet the ghost!"

"Who are you?"

"I'm Kimmey. The League of Scientists says, 'Hi!'"

CHAPTER 24

When she saw Kimmey run past, Malena snapped back to the present, mentally kicking herself for becoming distracted by the ghost in the pool. She raced up the bleachers, pushing between rows of screaming students as she climbed to the top. She had to see better. But since everyone around her was standing, she was too short to stay at ground level.

It was chaos. Students were running around, trying to either get closer to the freakishly shining pool or to get as far away from it as possible. All the water in the pool now glowed a bright green, and a thick fog hung over much of the water.

She stopped at the top of the bleachers and scanned the mob below her. Teachers were frantically trying to collect groups of screaming students. The teams from both schools mixed with friends and family, and a lot of people were running around the pool area itself, some slipping, some sliding, but luckily, none falling.

She saw Kimmey talking to Kyle, then turned to study the rest of the scene.

Hector was no help. Down at the other side of the pool, he was looking at the water and laughing. Knowing him, he probably thought the gigantic mess they'd made was hilarious.

John was just a few feet away from Hector. Holding the radio transmitter limply in one hand, he looked ill. He seemed to be paying more attention to his feet than to the excitement whirling around him.

Natsumi was down on the floor, and she and Malena made eye contact. Natsumi gave an exaggerated *what-do-we-do-now* gesture with both arms.

Malena held up a hand as she looked over the rest of the pool, checking out the crowd, trying to find anything out of the ordinary. Unfortunately, *everything* was out of the ordinary. The picture below her was filled with constant panicked movement, except for the League members … and *one other person*.

She waved frantically to Natsumi. Natsumi caught the signal, looked over, and instantly moved across the poolside area. She ran over to the East Rapids swim team towards Coach Warren.

Natsumi could see why he'd caught Malena's attention. The coach didn't look upset or surprised. He looked ashamed.

As she approached, he seemed to fold up in slow motion. He bent at the waist and sat down on a bench behind him. His head dropped down and he covered his face with his hand as if to shield his eyes from a bright light.

"Coach Warren?"

He looked up at her. His eyes were red-rimmed, and he had a haunted expression on his face.

"It shouldn't have…." He looked at her, but didn't really seem to see her. "I let it go too far. I should've stopped everything. I should have done something sooner."

Natsumi started to reply, but then stopped as she saw the coach's eyes focus on something behind her. She slowly turned and jumped, startled. Ms. Heida and Principal Murray stood there, and both were staring hard at Coach Warren.

"You'll have to excuse us," Principal Murray smiled at Natsumi with an overly polite, tight-lipped smile that looked more angry than friendly. "We need to talk to Coach Warren. Alone."

CHAPTER 25

Back at the Lab, the League clustered around the kitchen table.

"Okay," Kimmey said, smiling. "I probably shouldn't have rubbed it in. Kyle looked pretty mad after that. I wasn't very nice."

Malena said, "Well, no, it wasn't. And now he knows you're part of the League. But it's good you kept your cool through that whole thing. When our ghost appeared, we needed someone there watching the audience to see how they reacted. The right reaction showed us the guilty person, the one who created Casey's ghost."

"Where'd you get that idea, anyway?" Kimmey asked.

"It wasn't me," Malena replied. "It was Hector."

"Me?" Hector said. "Cool! What did I do?"

"You knew Kyle was acting weird, back when you first met him at the West Shore pool. It was the same when he saw our ghost—he acted different. If he was innocent, he would've been freaking out like everyone else."

"It's a good thing I was there, you know," said Kimmey. "After I dealt with Kyle, I looked for the rest of you. Hector, you were no use! Next time, try to help a little instead of pointing and laughing, okay?"

"He helped a lot, actually," Malena cut in, her eyes piercing. "We couldn't have done it without him. Actually, we couldn't have done it without *any* of us."

Kimmey sighed. "I guess. But John, what were *you* doing? I saw you sitting in a pool of green water after the ghost was released."

"After our ghost attacked those swimmers, I thought we were going to get expelled. My legs were shaking."

"You did it, though," Natsumi cut in kindly. "You really saved the day. You know that, right?"

John ducked his head. An embarrassed smile began to form. "I guess," he said.

"So, Kimmey," Malena began. "You saw Natsumi, right? And who she talked to? "

"There was another person?" Kimmey said. Her eyes turned sharp.

"There sure was," Natsumi said. "We weren't as fast as you, but Malena and I were watching too."

"Coach Warren." Malena said.

"Really?" Kimmey said, surprised. "I didn't see that."

"The principal and Ms. Heida were both there talking to him," Natsumi said, "Yelling at him. He looked miserable."

"Well," Malena said. "That makes sense. He knew Kyle scared Casey with that ghost, but he never said anything, even when Kyle gave him a flat tire the morning of the ghost."
"Did they fire him?" Kimmey asked.

Malena shook her head. “I talked to Ms. Heida after the fact. Apparently, Coach Warren’s sister is Kyle’s mom. They don’t have a lot of money, and swimming seems to be their plan for Kyle’s future. If West Shore won the meet against us, Kyle would be next in line for a scholarship to a prestigious swim summer camp. A lot of colleges recruit early at camps like that, and I guess that was how they were planning on securing Kyle’s future as a swimmer.”

“So, what happened to Kyle?” John asked. “Can he still swim?”

Malena met John’s eye, “Kyle was kicked off the team for the rest of his middle school career.”

Kimmey gasped, “But what about his future?”

Natsumi interjected, “You can’t secure your future by cheating. You have to work for it.”

“There aren’t any shortcuts,” Malena added, nodding.

“So, he really did create the ghost then, huh?” Hector asked.

Kimmey glanced at Malena. Then, turning to John, she said, “He says he didn’t. But his parents bought him some chemistry supplies a while ago.”

“Dry ice, too?” John asked.

“And fluorescein?” Natsumi added.

“His parents bought him dry ice, but they say they *didn’t* buy any fluorescein. He got it somehow, though, since he had orange fluorescein stains on his fingers, just like Kimmey.”

Natsumi shook her head. “Getting fluorescein is tough. You can’t just go to a store and buy it. I had to have my mom special order it for us. Who bought it for him?”

“I don’t know,” Malena admitted. “Maybe his parents *did* buy it for him, and it was the same stuff under a different name?”

"Either way," Hector said, "We solved our first major mystery: the mystery of the ghost in the water. Nice job, everyone!"

Everyone cheered. Malena raised a hand, immediately silencing everyone again. "But special thanks goes to our newest member."

John's heart lodged in his throat. He tried to think of something to say.

"... Houdini," Malena finished.

John was shocked for a moment, then started to laugh.

"Seriously," Malena said. "You did it, John. You were quick on your feet and saved the day."

Hector applauded loudly. He leaned over to John and said, "I'll never give you dead batteries again, John. I promise."

"Uh, thanks."

"You know," said Hector. "I talked with Casey at the meet, after everything happened and people were clearing out. He looked depressed, so I walked up and asked him if he was okay. He said he got in big trouble for swimming in the pool alone."

"I thought he swam alone there all the time," Kimmey said.

"Yeah, but they'd never known about it until the ghost incident. He doesn't even know if they'll let him swim anymore. And you know what else he told me? He said, 'I wanted the ghost to be real.'"

"He wanted a real ghost?" Kimmey said, annoyed. "What's that supposed to mean? After all the work we did? Seriously?

Hector laughed. "That's pretty much what I said, only I was nicer about it. Seriously, I think he was about to cry. So I told him, sure, there are ghosts."

"Why? I don't get it," Kimmey said.

"I said it to make him feel better. Come on; it had to be rough on him. He sees this thing that he really thinks is a ghost, he gets all excited about it, gets to tell everyone about it ... and then it turns out to be a stupid stunt by Kyle VanderJack."

Kimmey rolled her eyes. Hector continued, "So yeah, I told him that there *are* ghosts, but we eventually figure out what they *really* are. Then we get to move on to the *next* ghost, and see what makes *that* one tick."

Hector looked around and realized everyone was staring at him. He smiled, and shrugged. "Hey, that's how I see it. His ghost is our mystery. In the end, they're both the same thing."

"There's something you all should know," Malena said.

Everyone looked at her.

"When we formed the League of Scientists, I wanted a way for people to contact us. That's why Hector made the website. But we never really got any visitors."

"Uh oh," Hector said. "I think I know what's coming. You checked the mailbox?"

"Yeah, didn't *you*, Mr. Computer Expert?"

Hector didn't say another word. He yanked his laptop out of his backpack, flipped it open, and started typing furiously.

"What mailbox?" John asked Malena.

"Our website has a 'Contact Us' page, so people can reach us if they have any cases they need solved. We'd received exactly zero contact requests. No one wanted our help… until now. Kimmey, Kyle's big mouth really helped us. When you said 'Hi from the League of Scientists,' he must have told… well, everyone!"

Malena smiled. "Now that we've solved the mystery of the ghost in the water, we've got a few new cases, that is, if we want them."

"Whoa," Hector stopped typing and leaned back in his chair. "We've got more than a few. There are *twenty*! Sweet!"

"That's a lot of people asking for help," Malena said. "Though I don't know if there are really twenty cases. Some of them are likely just people messing around. Some people are really mad at us, probably because of Kyle." Malena glanced pointedly at Kimmey, who shrugged. "Some people think we were wrong and that ghosts exist. But others look like real people with cool mysteries. We can choose whatever we want. Like, did you guys know that East Rapids might have buried treasure? Or that a dead magician's magic is still alive? Or that there's a kid who thinks—"

"Hold on," John said. "We're pretty good with ghosts. Shouldn't we stick with ghost hunting?"

"Doesn't matter to me," grinned Malena. "I love ghosts, too, but I'm up for any mystery!"

John looked at the others. Hector, Kimmey, and Natsumi were hunched over the laptop, pointing at the screen and talking excitedly about the case list.

He smiled back at Malena.

***

The League sat and argued, trying to decide what their next case would be. For a few more minutes, the figure outside the window watched and listened.

It nodded to itself. It had seen enough. It knew enough.

Making sure to keep absolutely silent, it backed away, and left.

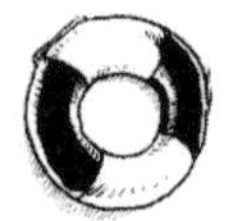

Glossary

Alpha
The first letter of the Greek alphabet. The symbols for Alpha are A and α.

Altimeter
A sensitive piece of equipment that is chiefly used in aircrafts for finding the differences above sea level, terrain, and or other reference points by a comparison of air pressures.

Amigo
The Spanish word for "friend."

Amphipods
A crustacean, such as a crab, lobster, shrimp or barnacle, from the chiefly marine order *Amphipoda.*

Anime
A style of Japanese comic book and video cartoon animation where the characters have large doe-like eyes.

Anpan
A type of Japanese sweet bread, most commonly filled with red bean paste. They are a healthy snack and a good alternative to donuts at breakfast.

Arigato
The Japanese phrase for "Thank you."

Barometer
An instrument that measures air pressure and predicts changes in the weather.

Beta
The second letter of the Greek alphabet. The symbols for Beta are B and β.

Binary
The code used to program computers and electronics, made up of combinations of the numbers 0 and 1.

Biodegradable
Capable of decaying through the action of living organisms like biodegradable paper or detergent.

Black Light
Long wave ultraviolet (uv) light emitted by lamps with special filters. The light glows purple.

Caesar Cipher
One of the simplest encryption techniques that involves substituting so that each letter in the message is replaced by a letter some fixed number of positions down the alphabet. The method is named after Julius Caesar who used it to send messages to his generals.
See Cipher and Substitution Cipher.

Calmate
The Spanish word for "calm down."

Carbon Dioxide
A colorless, odorless, noncombustible gas. It is composed of one atom of carbon and two atoms of oxygen.

Cipher
A code. A method of transforming a text to conceal its meaning.
See Caesar Cipher and Substitution Cipher.

Claro
The Spanish word for "clear."

Commensalism
A type of ecological relationship where one species benefits from the connection but the other species does not appear to be impacted negatively or positively.

Competition
A type of ecological relationship where organisms living in the same environment compete for available resources.

Computer Ports
A connection point on computers, modems, etc., that allow the transfer of data.

Cryptology
The study of codes, including writing and solving them.

Cuidado
The Spanish word for "careful."

Cytoplasm
The living material inside of a cell located outside of the nucleus.

Cytoskeleton
A microscopic network of protein filaments and tubules in the cytoplasm of many living cells, giving them shape and coherence.

Data
Facts or information usually used to calculate, analyze, or plan something.

Déjà vu
A French phrase that means "already seen" used to describe a feeling of having already experienced a situation.

Dezaato
Japanese word for dessert.

Dihydrogen Monoxide
A colorless and odorless chemical compound, also referred to as water. Dihydrogen can be written "H_2" and Monoxide can be written "O." When combined, it is H_2O — or water.

Dou itashimashite
The Japanese phrase for "You're welcome."

Dowsing
Two metal or wooden rods used to detect underground sources of water.

Dry Ice
The solid form of carbon dioxide, it is used primarily as a cooling agent for preserving frozen foods where mechanical cooling is unavailable. Dry ice sublimes at −109.3 °F (−78.5 °C) at Earth atmospheric pressures.

Environment
The surroundings and conditions in which organisms live and operate.

Flagellum
A microscopic, whip-like appendage that enables many protozoa, bacteria, spermatozoa, etc., to swim.

Fluorescein
An orange-red, crystalline, water insoluble solid that in alkaline solutions produces an orange color and an intense green color when mixed with water.

Fútbol
The Spanish word for "soccer."

Gamma
The third letter of the Greek alphabet. The symbols for Gamma are Γ and γ.

Gelatinous
Resembling gelatin or jelly in consistency.

Greek Alphabet
The alphabet used in Greek times, where Alpha, Beta, Gamma, etc. are used. It was derived from the earlier Phoenician alphabet and was in turn the ancestor of numerous other European and Middle Easter scripts, including Cyrillic and Latin.

HTML
Stands for Hyper Text Markup Language. It's the building block used to create web pages.

Hadopelagic
The bottommost layer of the oceanic zone, with depths greater than 6,000 meters.

Harry Houdini
A Hungarian-American illusionist and stunt performer, noted for his sensational escape acts.

¡Hasta luego!
The Spanish phrase for “See you later!”

Humidity
A measurement of the amount of water vapor in the air.

Infrared
A long wavelength beyond visible red that cannot be seen with the naked eye. It is often used to see things in the dark.

Ka
A word from ancient Egypt for the spirit of a human or god that survives after death and can be transferred to a statue of the person.

Kelp
A type of brown algae also referred to as seaweed.

Laser Pointer
A small handheld device that emits a very narrow, intense beam of visible light. They are generally used to highlight something of interest by illuminating it with a small bright spot of colored light.

LED
Acronym for Light Emitting Diode. These are tiny light bulbs that fit easily into an electrical circuit. Unlike ordinary incandescent bulbs, they don't have a filament that will burn out, and they don't get especially hot. The lifespan of an LED surpasses the life of an incandescent bulb by thousands of hours.

Lúcuma
A subtropical fruit native to the Andean valleys of Peru. It looks a bit like an avocado. It is celebrated for its amazing flavor and smooth-as-silk creamy texture

Mass
A measurement of the amount of matter.

Membrane
In living organisms, it separates sections of a cell. For example, the nucleus is separated from the rest of the cell by a membrane.

Mi amigo
The Spanish phrase for "my friend."

Military Time
Time measured in hours numbered up to twenty-four, for instance, 1:00 am is 0100 and 10:00 pm is 2200. This eliminates any confusion about whether a particular time is am or pm.

Mitochondria
Organelles in the cytoplasm of cells that produce energy for the cell.

Mutualism
A type of ecological relationship where both species benefit.

Nucleus
In atoms, it refers to the center of an atom where the charge is positive. In living cells, it refers to the part that contains most of the cell's genetic material.

Organelles
Structures that are part of a cell and control certain life activities.

Organism
Any uni-cellular or multi-cellular living thing.

Parasitism
A type of ecological relationship where one species benefits while the other species is negatively impacted.

Pixelated
When an image is magnified to see the points of light or pixels, causing the image to appear blurred.

Predation
A type of ecological relationship where one species, the predator, hunts organisms from another species, the prey.

Psi
The twenty-third letter of the Greek alphabet. The symbols for Psi are Ψ and ψ. Pronounced [sahy].

Pulse Monitor
A machine that checks a person's pulse.

¿Que pasa?
The Spanish phrase for "What's up?"

Radiation
The process in which energy is emitted as particles or waves.

Scientific Process
A method used by scientists to study the natural world. It usually involves formulating a hypothesis, which is a suggested explanation for an observation.

Señor
The word for "Mr." or "Sir" in Spanish.

Short Circuit
When the current in an electrical circuit is interrupted.

Soursop
The fruit of a flowering evergreen tree native to Central America, the Caribbean, and northern South America. It has a sweet tropical flavor with a hint of citrus sourness and a pleasing creamy texture.

Stagnant
Not flowing, active, changing or progressing.

Stimulus
Something that causes a reaction or response.

Sublimation
A change in state from solid directly to gas. Dry ice sublimates easily at room temperature.

Substitution Cipher
A method of encoding by where units of plaintext are replaced with ciphertext, according to a regular system; the "units" may be single letters (the most common), pairs of letters, triplets of letters, or mixtures of the different options.
See Cipher and Caesar Cipher.

Sundial
An instrument that indicates the time of day by using the position of the sun.

Symbiotic
The relationship between two different types of living things that depend on each other to survive.

Thermostats
A device that measures and, in most cases, adjusts the temperature.

Tomodachi
The Japanese word for "friend."

Ultraviolet
A type of light wave that is shorter than waves of violet light and cannot be seen by the human eye.

Vacuole
An organelle in cells that often stores food.

Vibration
The act of moving continuously and rapidly to and fro.

Visible
Capable of being seen.

Volcanologist
A scientist that studies the scientific study of volcanoes and volcanic phenomena.

Wavelength
The distance from one wave crest to the next.

WHOIS
Pronounced "who is," this is an Internet directory service, or question and response system, used to look up the names of people who own a domain name or a website.

List of contributors

Design:

Cover Design: Andrew Barthelmes, Peekskill, NY
Cover Art: Celia Kaiser, Grand Rapids, MI
Interior Art: Bob Al-Greene, New York City, NY
Layout: Melissa McClellan, Blacksburg, VA

Project Manager:

Dia L. Michels, Washington, DC

Production Editor:

Aislinn Boyter, Strafford, VA

Senior Editor:

Heather Kitt, Jefferson, IA
Melissa McClellan, Blacksburg, VA

Associate Editors:

Elizabeth Burns, Park City, UT
Michelle Goldchain, Washington, DC
Omid Khanzadeh, Stafford, VA
Megan Murray, Mitchellville, MD
Ashley Parker, Washington, DC
Benjamin Suehler, Washington, DC
Crystal Vogel, Washington, DC

Assistant Editors:

Noah Ballard, Lincoln, NE
Zoe Bernard, Oak Park, IL
Erin Friedlander, Fairfax, VA
Mae Hunt, Alexandria, VA
Michael Oshinsky, Washington, DC
Carlo Péan, Memphis, TN
Katy Reinsel, Fairfax, VA
Deborah Robertson, Baltimore, MD
Zoe Waltz, Indianapolis, IN

Teacher's Guide Lead Writer:

Sue Garcia, Spicewood, TX

Teacher's Guide Associate Writers:

Melissa McClellan, Blacksburg, VA
Joan Wagner, Saratoga Springs, NY

Index

A

Alpha, 28, 178, 181
Altimeter, 93, 178
Amigo, 11-12, 25, 146, 178, 183
Amphipods, 64-65, 178
Anime, 25, 178
Anpan, 111, 178
Arigato, 35, 178

B

Barometer, 93, 178
Beta, 28, 178, 181
Binary, 17-18, 24, 26, 178
Biodegradable, 151, 179
Black light, 117-123, 179

C

Caesar cipher, 17, 179
Calmate, 35, 179
Candelabra, 28
Carbon dioxide, 117, 179-180
Cipher, 17, 179, 184
Claro, 112, 179
Commensalism, 63, 179
Competition, 13, 56, 63, 69, 179
Computer ports, 93, 179
Cryptology, 64, 180
Cuidado, 44, 180
Cytoplasm, 21, 180, 183
Cytoskeleton, 20, 180

D

Data, 34-36, 40, 44-45, 67, 179-180
Déjà vu, 80, 180
Dezaato, 11, 180
Dihydrogen monoxide, 109-111, 180
Dou itashimashite, 35, 180
Dowsing, 42, 140, 180
Dry ice, 89, 118- 119, 122, 125, 147-148, 152, 156, 158, 163-164, 173, 180, 184

E

Environment, 64-65, 151, 179, 181

F

Flagellum, 20, 129, 181
Fluorescein, 120-121, 124, 146-149, 151-152, 156, 158, 163-164, 166, 173, 181
Fútbol, 41, 181

G

Gamma, 28, 181
Gelatinous, 58, 79, 181
Greek alphabet, 27, 178, 181, 183

H

Hadopelagic, 64-64, 181
¡Hasta luego! 15, 182
Houdini, Harry, 126, 148, 181
HTML, 13, 181
Humidity, 34, 79, 182

I

Infrared, 117, 182

K

Ka, 182
Kelp, 68, 182
Khufu, 17

L

Laser pointer, 117, 182
LED, 118, 161, 182
Lúcuma, 11, 182

M

Mass, 56, 182
Membrane, 20, 182
Mi amigo, 12, 25, 183
Military time, 44, 183
Mitochondria, 20, 183
Mutualism, 62, 183

N

Nucleus, 20, 180, 182-183

O

Organelles, 21, 183
Organism, 63, 179, 181-183

P

Parasitism, 63, 183
Pixelated, 52-53, 183
Predation, 61, 181
Psi, 27-28, 183
Pulse monitor, 93, 184

R

Radiation, 117, 184

Q

Que Pasa, 14, 184

S

Scientific process, 41-42, 184
Señor, 93, 184
Short circuit, 31, 184
Soursop, 11, 184
Stagnant, 72, 184
Stimulus, 93, 185
Sublimation, 119, 180, 184
Substitution cipher, 17, 184
Sundial, 91, 185
Symbiotic, 62-63, 185

T

Telepathy, 75, 83
Thermostat, 93, 185
Tomodachi , 11, 185

U

Ultraviolet, 90, 117, 179, 185

V

Vacuole, 21, 185
Vibration, 34, 36, 40, 185
Visible, 72, 81, 90, 101, 116-117, 182, 185
Volcanologist, 34, 185

W

Wavelength, 90, 117, 182, 185
WHOIS, 143, 185

About Science, Naturally!

Science, Naturally is an independent press located in Washington, DC. We are committed to increasing science and math literacy by exploring and demystifying these topics in entertaining and enlightening ways. Our products are filled with interesting facts, important insights, and key connections across the curriculum.

We engage readers using both fiction and nonfiction strategies to make potentially intimidating subjects intriguing and accessible to scientists and mathematicians of all ages.

We are gratified by the recognition and awards we have received from the education, literacy and parenting communities. All our books have earned the coveted "Recommends" designation from the National Science Teachers Association and our math books have been praised by the National Council of Teachers of Mathematics. Our newest science mysteries book was selected for the "Outstanding Science Trade Books for Students K-12" list. All of our books have been designated as valuable supplemental resources for schools, extended learning programs, and home education alike.

Our content aligns with the Next Generation Science Standards and supports the Common Core State Standards. Articulations to these, as well as many others, are available on our website.

All of our publications are available as E-books and foreign language editions include Spanish (and Spanish/English bilingual), Chinese, Korean, Hebrew, and Dutch—with more to come! Select titles are also available in Braille.

Science, Naturally books are distributed by National Book Network in the United States and abroad. For more information about our publications, to request a catalog, to be added to our mailing list, to explore joining our team, or to learn more about becoming a *Science, Naturally* author, please give us a call or visit us online.

We hope that you enjoy reading our books as much as we enjoy creating them!

Bridging the gap between the blackboard and the blacktop

Science, Naturally!®
725 8th Street, SE
Washington, DC 20003
202-465-4798 • Fax: 202-558-2132
Toll-free: 1-866-SCI-9876 (1-866-724-9876)
Info@ScienceNaturally.com
www.ScienceNaturally.com
/ScienceNaturally @SciNaturally

Check Out Other Award Winning Titles From Science, Naturally!

One Minute Mysteries series

65 Mysteries You Solve With Math
65 Mysteries You Solve With Science
65 MORE Mysteries You Solve With Science

---

101 Things... series

101 Things Everyone Should Know About Math
101 Things Everyone Should Know About Science

Blended Stem Fiction

Innovators in Action! Leonardo da Vinci Gets a Do-Over